Elinor and Marianne

A Sequel to

SENSE AND SENSIBILITY

Also by Emma Tennant

The Colour of Rain
The Crack
Hotel de Dream
Wild Nights
Alice Fell
Queen of Stones
Woman Beware Woman
Black Marina
The Bad Sister
The Adventures of Robina
Two Women of London: The Strange Case of Ms Jekyll
and Mrs Hyde
Sisters and Strangers
Faustine
Tess
Pemberley
An Unequal Marriage

(*For Children*)

The Boggart
The Ghost Child

Elinor and Marianne

A *Sequel to*

SENSE AND SENSIBILITY

Emma Tennant

with illustrations by Nicola Leader

SIMON & SCHUSTER

LONDON · SYDNEY · NEW YORK · TOKYO · SINGAPORE · TORONTO

First published in Great Britain by Simon & Schuster Ltd, 1996
A Viacom Company

The right of Emma Tennant to be identified as author of this
work has been asserted in accordance with sections 77 and 78
of the Copyright, Designs and Patents Act 1988

Simon & Schuster Ltd
West Garden Place
Kendal Street
London W2 2AQ

Simon & Schuster of Australia Pty Ltd
Sydney

A CIP catalogue record for this book is available from
the British Library

ISBN 0-684-81626-1

Typeset in Sabon by
Palimpsest Book Production Limited, Polmont, Stirlingshire
Printed and bound in Great Britain by
Butler & Tanner, Frome & London

For Jane Miller
with love

From Marianne Brandon to Elinor Ferrars

The thirteenth of February 1812

My dear Sister,

   I write to tell you that your company is much missed at Delaford and that neither Colonel Brandon nor I will countenance your staying away from us for as much as one week longer.

   How unfortunate it has been for all of us, that urgent matters connected with poor Edward's family have kept you from Dorsetshire! The cruel ironies of life have given you a husband with a new parish to attend to; a Parsonage which my husband wishes at his own expense to repair; and a village of puzzled parishioners who cannot see when their priest shall come amongst them and help them mend their ways.

Apart from all this, I may add, a visit from our half-brother John and his wife, Fanny, is threatened at the beginning of Spring. How am I to sustain the wounding remarks of a sister-in-law, her repeated attempts to seize hold of our mother's china (for Mama will come from Barton at the same time – the journey from Honiton is not so great and she thinks it right to pay her respects to her stepson and his wife on the occasion of their coming from Norland to visit us); and the sulks and boredom of our youngest sister, Margaret, who must for propriety's sake accompany Mama? How am I to bear all this without you, my dear, my very dearest Elinor – whose calm and composure will bring tranquillity in the wildest of storms – and I confess my heart beats with apprehension already! . . .

No, Elinor, you *must* come. Edward, who has expressed his resolve to devote his life to the service of others, must understand your need to be ensconced in your home and no longer at the mercy of relatives who have shown you precious little charity since his choice of you as his bride. Edward, if I may venture to say so, my dear, finds himself on the brink of becoming selfish; or if it is not that, then the wretched dominance of Mrs. Ferrars over her son has most unsuitably asserted itself on the occasion of your visit – which should, at the very least, be paid with all the show of independence from parental interference that marriage must produce. This is the time, kind, sweet Elinor, for you to encourage a little spirit in your husband: he shall not be instructed to go hither and thither by his Mama any more – and particularly should not be encouraged to linger in a place where his brother's wife, Lucy, holds the heart and affections of Mrs. Ferrars and very likely dictates from behind the throne the orders she gives.

A new life awaits you both here, my dearest Sister. Speak firmly to the new Parson of Delaford, and inform him that the generosity of his patron, Colonel Brandon, begins to wear thin. The living here was granted to Edward by a man who pitied the poverty of a son cut off from his family and without ambition or desire to succeed in the world; but for how much longer will the glow of satisfaction attendant on so selfless a gesture endure, when the Parsonage remains empty and the papers you chose, dear Elinor, having been found to be unavailable at either Yeovil or Weymouth, have not yet been replaced? Do we merely distemper? Will not the place look cold, with no more than a coat of paint to hide the deficiencies in masonry and woodwork alike? The estate carpenter stands idle, awaiting your instructions on the small parlour . . . the chimneys are swept, but show no friendly sign of smoke to rouse me from my long reveries in the upper drawing-room of the Mansion-house . . . There was a shrubbery discussed, but it is not ordered until such time as Mr. and Mrs. Edward Ferrars determine its exact placing at the Parsonage.

Now I shall tease you no longer, and will confide to you instead my excellent ruse for postponing the visit of our brother John and Fanny – though I would not deceive Mama, as you know, for anything in the world.

I have informed them that winter has us in its grip down here. Do you recall our childhood winters in Sussex, Elinor – when snow came down on the roof of Norland and the milking pails were quite froze over – when the dirty lanes I would find so picturesque – while you thought them dirty and muddy and little more – turned to glissades of ice, where children tumbled and fell? The downs with their great weight of snow, stayed above the park and might engulf us, in the great long hush of winter . . . this is the weather we knew there as children – and there are times, I confess, when I dream of it here.

Well, I have writ to brother John and prayed that he

and Fanny wait for the first signs of Spring, before they come across the country to visit us at Delaford. By the time they come, dear Elinor, you will be here and I know happiness and contentment will reign at Mansion-house and Parsonage alike.

In the meantime, I shall tell you the truth, dear Sister. Yesterday, climbing on Lewesdon Hill, I found the first violets. They made a touch of dark purple in the frosty grass on the lane that winds upwards to the great beech forest . . . where we shall walk so often, my dearest Elinor. And on the way down my happy gaze picked on the first primrose . . . and then another clump, pale and brave and growing just at the margins of your own untended garden!

Oh, Elinor, Spring has come to Delaford – as it has no doubt for Mama at Barton, for Devonshire is just as advanced as we are here. There are skies so misty blue they presage the first hedge sparrow's egg; the air is often warm so I walk out to the yew arbour with little more around me than a shawl. A frog calls to another on the canal – which is horribly green with slime, and McAllister the gardener says must be cleaned out before it stinks in high summer.

Birds sing in cherry trees where the very first buds, still clinging to the bare branches, show like the eyes of new-born creatures on the bark . . .

All Nature brings forth, my dear Sister – and only I, for no reason that Dr. Davis can construe, do not. On some days, when it is fine enough to walk to the old mulberry tree, I go to sit on the ancient bench around it and pray for the child that will bring fulfilment to our union. I must confess this lack to you – for I have never gone without telling you of every feeling and sensation in my heart – while you, dear Sister, have so often and so long concealed all your own inner joy or agony.

I believe, as I have never believed anything in my life

before, that your coming, and the advent of Spring at Delaford, will grant me my dearest wish. Do not disappoint me, Sister – come soon, before the first daffodil and the cuckoo, so strong a feature of the Marshwood Vale and far-flung hills, makes further mockery of your affectionate sister

Marianne

From Elinor Ferrars to Marianne Brandon

The nineteenth of February 1812

My dear Sister,

It is impossible for you to guess, my sweet Marianne, at the pleasure I felt on receiving a letter from you. That so long has passed since we have corresponded must be my fault entirely; your own dear nature is such that a day without a word of friendship appears a month to you; and if it had not been for the series of misadventures – nay, disasters – which have befallen us here, I would have ensured you a daily dose of my affection, even to the point of boredom on your part.

That I have not recounted all to you has been due to the faults in my own character. It is true, as you say, that I am ever wont to conceal rather than confide – and this characteristic, as has on many occasions proved to be the case – has caused misunderstanding, even mistrust, from those closest in my family circle. But old habits are hard to break; there was much to do here, when the blow fell; and to see poor Edward's misery was to make the impulse to fetch pen and ink appear a crass one. Some suffering can be borne only in silence: in respect to Edward and his mother, if not to his younger brother Robert, I stayed my hand each time I thought of you – and this was many times in the course of each day – and I resolved to wait until our installation at Delaford before burdening my dear sister and my new brother with an account as sordid as it is sad.

Now, however, I must wait no longer. I feel very sensibly your own puzzlement at our long absence. I grieve the lack of confident anticipation that must arise amongst the people of the village of Delaford – who, finding themselves recipients of all the sweetness and compassion of which I know you capable – find a mistress of the Mansion-house who begs her husband (as they must believe) to procure a living for her sister's husband, only to discover the Parson and his wife have apparently no intention in the world of being there.

And what must Colonel Brandon think? It appears to him undoubtedly that Edward Ferrars, cast out by his family when he felt bound to continue with his engagement to Lucy Steele, is now better provided for by his mother on his marriage to a Miss Dashwood than would have been at first the case – for his clear attachment to me, as you must recall, Sister, was at first much disapproved of by all the Ferrars family, not excluding our sister-in-law, Fanny.

Now, Colonel Brandon must feel, the living at Delaford is no longer for Edward the difference between shame and penury, and the possibility of a respectable existence. To come to the Parsonage, for all the inducements which your own dear presence at Delaford will afford, must appear to your husband an irritation to Edward rather than a happy necessity. There are other, better ways of passing the time than living on two hundred pounds a year in the depths of Dorsetshire! Edward (or so Colonel Brandon must think) may decide against the Church, has perhaps in his improved circumstances committed himself to politics as his mother had ever wished him to do, or wishes merely to travel or to hunt. The kind Colonel, so recently entered into the marital bliss of which, dear Marianne, he had frankly despaired before you had the good sense and the good fortune to accept him, must wonder at this thorn, however small and insignificant, in the flesh of his contented union with you. Shall Edward Ferrars prove a disappointment to the diocese, an emblem of the faulty judgement of his new brother at the Mansion-house?

These considerations, as I so clearly see, must produce just what we both least desire: that is to say, a coolness between our husbands. And that, dear Marianne, there must never be. So it is, with a heavy heart, that I pick up my pen at last; and I give you my word of honour that we had expected to be back with you at least six weeks ago, to see in a New Year which at that time seemed to promise nothing but joy and fulfilment. I shall endeavour to describe to you the chapter of accidents – or misfortunes, each as grisly and inescapable as the last, which have overtaken poor Edward's family.

I will break the worst of the news quite straight, dear Sister: Ferrars Hall is up for sale. Mrs. Ferrars and Robert are rendered penniless (and Edward, it must be said, suffers the least, for his small trust, placed outside the family with a lawyer of his own choosing, cannot be broached).

Robert Ferrars and his actions are responsible for this sorry state of affairs – though his mother will still not believe it of her younger son and her favourite, I regret to say.

You will recall Robert, whom we discovered to be as vain as a coxcomb (how uncharitable I am become, as a parson's wife!) on the occasion of our season at the London house of Mrs. Jennings. (But, dear Marianne, I do not wish to dwell on that time in your life for a good reason, and I ask only that you recollect how expensive Robert was set to be; how I told you of his spending an hour at least in Bond-street choosing a toothpick case set in diamonds and rubies &c., and how surprised we all were at his engagement to the penniless Lucy Steele, when the Hon. Miss Morton and her thirty thousand pounds were mercilessly dangled before him after dear Edward chose me to be his wife.)

Robert, then, is the architect of his family's misfortune. His grand investment schemes, which took in many innocent people (for Robert, as the son of Mrs. Ferrars, was considered the very last word in solid worth and incapable of misrepresenting a financial situation) all came to nothing, when it was discovered that the buildings that were to rise in Bath and London and elsewhere had no more than a paper and pencil reality, and no foundations in the soil; and the 'sunken treasure' off the coast of Scotland, the 'Ferrars gold', as was much trumpeted abroad, was discovered, on investigation by a board of Scottish bankers concerned at claims made on the subject of this fabulous treasure, to be no more than a collapsed trawler, with a ton of mud and old fishing tackle, secured to the bottom of the ocean by a marlin-spike.

After this, things went from bad to worse. The house in Park-street (where you will recall Mrs. Ferrars as she received her guests in her queenly fashion) was found to be mortgaged up to – indeed beyond – its current value in the event of the necessity of its sale; and in an unpleasant rush, after Robert's wife, Lucy, attempted to creep in overnight before the sale to seize her mother-in-law's jewels and her own hats, the bailiffs came and evicted Mrs. Robert Ferrars – with disastrous attendant publicity – from the premises. Since when, it is needless for me to recount, any shred of trust in Robert or his ventures vanished as surely and permanently as the 'Ferrars gold'.

If all that were not enough, my dear Sister, it transpired that Robert's debts could not be repaid – and even then not all of them – without the sale of Ferrars Hall, estates which have been in the family since the time of William the Norman King, or so Robert and his mother have so frequently vouchsafed. The furniture went at auction last week; and you may imagine how sorely tempted I became, to confide all this dreadful tale of woe to you – for we sleep now on mattresses lent by estate workers still loyal to the Ferrars name – though they, too, have been appallingly mistreated, their cottages damp and unrepaired and their wages several years in arrears. Their trust in 'Master Robert' cannot be thought to endure long, now we have neither plate nor chairs to sit down on; and the land agent, who had been just a few weeks ago a model of subservience and respect, has declared that the river cannot be fished nor the land 'poached' for game while the trustees organise the sale. (It is thought that a local merchant, Mr. Butts by name, will purchase the property in its entirety, and it is hard to say which grieves my mother-in-law the most – the loss of the Ferrars estates, or its acquisition by a man who had previously supplied her with pig manure for her ornamental gardens and specimen trees.)

There is still worse, my dearest Sister, and it is only right that you should know all before we come south to the pleasantness of Dorsetshire and the peace and harmony for which we yearn.

Mrs. Ferrars, as of course we have been made only too aware since John's marriage, is mother to Fanny, John's wife and our sister-in-law. She proclaims it at least a hundred times a day. 'My Fanny will save me!' – so she declared over and over, as one sideboard or inlaid cabinet or other was carried from the room and set on a cart on the sweep outside. 'She has told me often enough there are cottages to be had at Delaford – there is nothing at Norland, she and John are so very hard up, you know, after giving away so

11

much to John's sisters' – Yes, Marianne, I know you will smile at that – 'but in Dorset, though Colonel Brandon has only two thousand pounds a year, there is a tidy estate,' and Robert informs her the Colonel's land has excellent timber, on the subject of which he has an interesting plan of investment. He is confident his scheme will interest his host greatly when they all go south to visit you.

Yes, dear Sister, you have probably guessed if I know you aright, how Mrs. Ferrars intends to furnish this cottage she has with such facility built in her imagination to stand in a small park on your land, with enough room, as Robert has already assured her, to entertain eighteen couples.

'Fanny has told me,' said Mrs. Ferrars, 'of the wicked removal by your mother of all the china, linen and some choice pieces of furniture from Norland, shortly after the death of her husband, Henry.' It appears Fanny then went on to inform Mrs. Ferrars that our mother had stolen these items, which rightly belonged to Norland, and thus to John, the heir – 'so soon!' said Fanny, ' – it was a disgrace!' Thus Mrs. Ferrars – to *me*, Marianne! I feel you boil with indignation as I write this (and it is indeed one of the reasons I have delayed in writing to you, for you informed me in your last letter, if you recall, that you hoped to find yourself in a delicate condition, and I did not wish to upset you at such a time).

So Mrs. Ferrars is now persuaded that poor Mama's china and few pieces – which were from the first intended to be hers, and which our father expressly stated should remain with her after his death – are 'stolen' and must be returned to Fanny, who will then in turn present them to her mother for her new and magnificent cottage on your land! Is it not beyond anything? And that Mama should be accused of departing with her own property 'so soon' – why, it was Fanny who insisted on taking possession of Norland before Papa was cold in his grave; and how grieved we all were; even John, as I recall, felt shame at the indecent haste manifested by his wife.

So, my dear, my very dear Sister, I write with news that cannot bring you anything, I fear, but disquiet and grief. You may even, when thinking of your desire to have us so close to you, reconsider the offer of the Parsonage at Delaford altogether – or Colonel Brandon may, for I have learnt that he is one of Robert Ferrars's creditors. The Colonel has shown the good breeding of which we were immediately aware on first meeting him at Barton Park, by desisting from pressing for repayment of the loan – and this, doubtless, for family reasons – but for how much longer will the owner of Delaford, with all the considerations an estate must involve, wish to support the indigent members of the Ferrars family? He has offered a living to Edward; and he has lent money, without once stooping to mention the fact, to his brother Robert. It strikes cold at my heart to hear Mrs. Ferrars's proposals that he house *her* as well; and I hope to gain the wisdom from you at the earliest opportunity that no such cottage as she has dreamt of, can possibly exist at Delaford. (Oh Sister, how uncharitable I feel once again, but I fear that Mrs. Ferrars's fantasy may take possession of her altogether, as she today threatened to visit poor Mama, and to call on Mama's cousin Sir John Middleton at Barton Park at the time she comes to claim the furniture and china – oh dear!)

Dearest Marianne, to summon to my mind your happiness and tranquillity is my greatest balm. Poor Edward sends you, as I do a hundred times more, the most sincere affection. And you must forgive me that I do not enquire which delightful and improving books the Colonel has given you to read, since we were last together. *Marmion*, perhaps, for I

heard him mention it when we were last at Delaford, and he looked so thoughtfully and tenderly at you as he spoke . . .
Yours very affectionately,

Elinor Ferrars

From Marianne Brandon to Elinor Ferrars

The twenty-first of February

My beloved, my dearest Sister – my heart is still beating with agitation at the sight of your sweet and familiar handwriting this morning – and the dreadful tidings it conveys. How bitter cold you must be at Ferrars Hall, now it is dismantled – does this letter even reach you there? In the name of God, Elinor, forward to me a posting address in the event that you are all put out in that inhospitable clime – you were ever prone to catch a cold and for the rheum to reach down to the chest – though the admission of ill-health could scarce be prised from you at the time. Mama would be so anxious to think you in peril, and all in the service of the wretched Mrs. Ferrars! Why, she does not deserve so much as the time of day from you, my beloved Sister; and I know it is for your husband that you sustain such discomfort and unpleasantness. In that watery, low land where the nearest neighbour to Ferrars Hall is the King of Denmark (as I recall Mrs. Ferrars was wont to boast), the wind must be bitter at this time of year. There can be no sign of Spring, such as we have here at Delaford.

I fear for you, Sister, and urge you to come south to the Parsonage with as much haste as you can summon in the circumstances. I will not countenance your insinuations that Christopher and I tire of the prospect of seeing Edward as spiritual leader of the good souls of this parish – and as for the papers for the house, we have discovered a fine place in Bridport, never known to either of us before, whence the latest designs may be ordered and supplied without delay. As you have yourself been so much delayed, I shall take the liberty of choosing a pretty garlanded design for you, with hearts and lovebirds in a twist of forget-me-nots – for the north-facing bedroom you and Edward will wish to occupy (the front bedroom is low-ceilinged and too hot in summer for comfort: so I determined when roaming those unoccupied rooms where I have long awaited your loving presence, so close to me). You will receive the sun after midday in the parlour, dearest Elinor – and there I envisage you greeting callers and stooping over your desk, engaged in a letter to Mama or a matter of the parish. In time you may wish to build a conservatory – they are all the rage at present – but now I know myself indiscreet once more, for out has come Colonel Brandon's latest generous offer, to improve your hours of repose at Delaford – and I did swear to him that I would not reveal it to you until after you had returned! Christopher has the matter quite in hand – there! I have said it all – but your misfortune in Norfolk and your kindness and forbearance with the wretched Ferrars family have made it impossible for me to remain silent on the subject of the conservatory.

Think of the peaches and grapes that shall ripen there, Elinor, and the blooms accustomed to the climes of Italy! How you shall sit of a May evening, with Edward at work on his sermon, and the two of you as enamoured as the lovebirds I chose for your bedroom walls from the warehouse at Bridport . . .

The matter of Mrs. Ferrars's future accommodation brought me a pang of compassion for the poor woman, I confess – but as you must be aware, Elinor, there is no question of there being a cottage here; and there is no question, either, of my approaching Colonel Brandon on the subject. (I could not be sure, dearest Sister, whether you did not in some part feel it desirous that she should settle in Dorsetshire near you, if only for the reason that she has so long occupied a great part of the affections of her son and your husband, Edward. It would not be unlike you to forfeit your own feelings in order to gratify *his*; and in all probability you have given your word, albeit unwillingly, that you will enquire of your sister and your new brother of the possibility of a home for Mrs. Ferrars and her household.)

This cannot be, my Elinor, for a reason that may appear strange to you, who find yourself in circumstances so straitened that every nicety of feeling must go out of the window, along with the fine furnishings of Ferrars Hall.

It is simply that I cannot bring myself to ask any favour of my Christopher. It would be impossible for me to broach the subject of dependants settling here: I could not bring the words out, were I to lose (God forbid!) even your love and affection, and be doomed to solitude and misery for the rest of my days.

You will imagine – but do not do so too hastily! – that

17

there is a dearth of affection between my husband and myself. You will assume that I know myself to be as once I was: a headstrong girl who found Colonel Brandon too old at a little past five and thirty; made ill-judged jests on the subject of his fondness for flannel waistcoats, to keep away the rheumatism; and confess myself now the dissatisfied child bride of a much older man.

You would be mistaken, Elinor – indeed you would. It is true that, at first, we seemed to have one belief in common, and little else – and that belief, as you may well recall, was in the lasting quality of first romantic attachments, and of the improbability of any second attachment approaching the depth of feeling of the first.

Both Colonel Brandon and I, as you also know only too well, had suffered disastrous first attachments. Christopher had loved his orphaned cousin, who was cruelly married to his brother against her will, miserably ill-treated and forced to run away, only to be seduced and abandoned and die in a sponging-house, robbed of fortune, beauty and hope. I, as we do not wish to speak of, even between ourselves – and I have taken a silent vow never to do so – was desperately in love with Willoughby, a jilt and a scoundrel, and came close to losing my own life in the fever which succeeded the intelligence of his abandonment of a tender love for me.

So both Christopher and I were wary in the extreme, at first. He would persevere with his plan to educate me (for, as I can freely admit, my head was filled only with spectral emanations, phantasmagoria and all the wild imaginings *The Mysteries of Udolpho* and books of that like provide for the untutored mind); and I was grateful to accept the learning, wisdom and advice that were the legacy of my husband's increase in years and experience over mine.

Then, dear Sister, both Christopher and I began to demonstrate to each other that, while still believing it impossible

18

to love by halves, there was indeed room for another love to grow up beside the shadow of the former one. A different kind of gift from books was brought to me . . . gifts which showed my husband's appreciation of my sensibilities and love of Nature: a fern, a spray of leaves when the autumn winds brought chestnut branches crashing to the ground; a sketchbook (for he would have me emulate you and repay my debt to Nature with the delicate pencil strokes of which you – and never I – can dream of being capable).

More than this, one day I was to find a strange, shrouded object in the upper drawing-room – No, Elinor! I do not return to my belief in ghosts and other unworldly apparitions: it was a harpsichord! 'My dear Marianne,' came in the Colonel's neat hand (for it is not possible to forget he is a military man; all is excessively neat and tidy at Delaford) 'my dear child, you must forgive so impetuous a gesture as this. But, as you play exceedingly well, and every family in the country is already eager to hear you at the piano, I introduce the harp to Delaford so that you may acquire the skills of performing upon it for my selfish pleasure alone.'

Was this not sweet, Sister? It is the longest collection of words uttered by my husband since our marriage; and even if writ and not spoke, a signal of his desire to become the joy of my heart, the charm of my life, and the comfort of my soul.

I have practised on the harpsichord today: I improve but slowly, and as the Colonel is so many hours of the day away from my side, the excruciating twanging is heard only by the servants and by my faithful spaniel, Fluff.

I fear I do not have it in me to play the harp, Elinor: but I would not for the world confide this to my dear spouse.

All this – and I have not told you how I grieve for the misfortunes that befall your new family – and therefore, for never was there a kinder-hearted being in the world, yourself. I speak, I recognise, only of me, of Marianne, of my contentments and inadequacies – and not once do I consider the very real privations of my own, my beloved sister! But I yearn for you, above all others, to understand my predicament in my married life – viz. that I am given so much and can return so pitifully little. It is because I have ever confided all to you that I describe the Colonel's painful efforts to transform himself, at his advanced stage of life, from a man who had long considered himself a man incapable of loving again to my husband and fully half of a fulfilling union.

It is for that reason, when December marries May, that I cannot blight the first blooms of an unaccustomed tenderness by demanding more of dear Christopher than he already gives. I know you comprehend my delicacy on the subject, Sister; and I know, though your own kind heart is too sensible of cruelties commonly meted out by families to agree with me in so many words – that the absolute refusal of any cottage for Mrs. Ferrars on the Delaford estate may come secretly as a relief to you.

The time has surely come for Edward to free himself from the dominance of his mother; and now she is no longer rich, she will turn exceedingly tiresome.

Admit, if only in your most private thoughts, Elinor, that this is true. And I beg you, do not fret yourself over Mama and her possessions, all safe with her at Barton Cottage, as they now have been for many a long year.

Everything Mama has was left to her in our father's will . . . How well I remember the green lacquer chest, and how we would dream we had sailed to China when we climbed inside it . . . how I tried to hide little Margaret there and how cross Nurse became when I would not tell her whence emanated those blood-curdling cries . . .

Dearest, most adored Elinor – you are fatigued and tried beyond endurance by your sojourn at Ferrars Hall, first intended as a wedding trip before Edward takes up his duties as parson here – and extended unbearably as a result of the knavery of Robert Ferrars, whom I have ever disliked as much as his scheming wife Lucy. You are quite mistaken in thinking that our brother would permit Mrs. Ferrars, even if she *is* the mother of Fanny, to approach poor Mama on the subject of her plate and porcelain. Why, John was shocked that Fanny was so quick to get in to Norland, and he will be doubly on guard, this time, to ensure Fanny's mother does not try to take anything from Mama. Robert is an acknowledged criminal – for he must be disgraced as well as bankrupt – and doubtless the blood that runs in all their veins, not excluding Fanny's, will need curbing in future before another opportunity arises for it to assert itself.

Oh Elinor, I did not intend any reference to your dear husband, Edward! He and he alone has stood for the honour of the Ferrars family. He cares not for material things; would not cheat anybody for anything in the world; and was prepared even to stand by his engagement to Lucy Steele rather than act dishonourably . . . and while so violently in love with you! (I am mistaken in my words here, I believe, for Edward cannot be violent in anything. He is a gentle soul.) I only pray that Lucy, who married to the surprise of everyone the brother she assumed would take all Mrs. Ferrars's estate, does not come down to Delaford once you are both installed here, in pursuit of Edward's memories of his feelings towards her, and your own generous hospitality, now the money is all gone and the ancient Norfolk lands all dispersed too. I shall certainly not make her welcome here. You should take account of that, Elinor – for it may assist you in refusing her the haven she is likely to beg of you.

Now I must cease, for I hear the return of the hunt:

the meet was at Delaford this morning and I pleaded a sick headache in order to be able to write to you, dearest Sister.

I send you a box of stockings and two garters, fortunately ready knit and never worn by me, to keep off the cold and pernicious mists that rise from the sea at Wells and Burnham Overy Staithe at this time of year.

I hear my dear husband's tread on the stair. And as I write this I feel myself already close to tears at having to disappoint poor Christopher once more.

For it seems Colonel Brandon is so little acquainted with women's dispositions, that the slightest headache or ailment on my part is at once heralded by him (albeit with the utmost tact and courtesy!) as proof that I am at last with child.

He yearns for a child, Elinor . . . as I do, for I know we would be more fully at ease with each other if this binding and wonderful gift from God were to be bestowed upon us. Yet once more, I shall have to intimate to the Colonel that this is not to be . . .

Elinor, my blessed angel, I have unburdened myself too long. You, I daresay, pray also for children – but, correctly, you will not state in public, or even in private correspondence, where your hopes and prayers may lie.

Certainly, for us to have a child each at the Mansion-house and the Parsonage would be very heaven. Sometimes I believe I hear their running feet, the sound of laughter in a far-off room.

Did I inform you Sir John Middleton is bent on giving a ball for our sister Margaret at Barton Park? It will be at Midsummer; we will all go down there together from Delaford and stay with Mama at Barton Cottage – and who knows, by then we may be blessed with the knowledge of happy events to come . . .

Write to me as soon as you receive this, I beg of you.

Come ahead of Edward and stay with me here in the Mansion-house. But come . . .

Your devoted sister,

Marianne

From Marianne Brandon to Elinor Ferrars

The twenty-third of February

My dear Elinor,

Before you have time to reply to me – but then, you so seldom do! – here at last is news that is worth the swiftest return: I am informed by Dr. Davis, who was last night called up to the Mansion-house by Colonel Brandon (he fears so for my health, too much so, I fear, since my illness at Mrs. Palmer's in that fateful year), that I am indeed with child! I have been mistaken – or rather I have bled some but not enough to lose the precious infant altogether – I am two months into pregnancy, Elinor!

Oh, Sister, this is momentous news. My love is all yours as I write these words. Christopher is silent still – for, poor

25

man, he cannot speak when he feels and I believe, with all his formal utterances, that he cannot feel when he speaks. It is you I need now, as never before in my life, Elinor . . . for all the loving care you lavished on me when I was brought down with putrid fever at Cleveland returns to me so forcefully now. You, and you alone, my dearest, most beloved Sister, will keep this child within me, living, awaiting the happy hour when our faces bend low over the cradle together and our smiles unite, to bring happiness to this new miracle of life.

Christopher I include, of course – I see you frown at the marriage I have made between two sisters when husbands must be the first to express their joy and felicitations in the happy event of a new arrival in the family.

But Elinor, I can scarce believe this: Colonel Brandon announced his intentions at breakfast this morning, when the intelligence that he is to know the great joy of fatherhood came only late last night – that he is to travel today to his estates in Wales and cannot postpone the arrangements he has made there, even for this!

There has been poaching of the salmon at Brecon, it appears, and cattle gone overnight. A grave matter, indeed – but I see now, with a greater clarity than I have known before, that land and stock are of greater importance to Colonel Brandon than his own future child.

How can he, Elinor, how can he? A new housekeeper, a Mrs. Jenkins, is to come from Taunton; there are servants enough in the house; and Dr. Davis lives in the village of Delaford and will send even to Bath if there are complications; but, dear Sister, I dream only of gallows and gibbets, of poor lads hanging for their crimes against Colonel Brandon's land. I see my child affected; a babe born with a cord about its neck; a grotesquely swollen lip &c., &c. – for all that Christopher assures me I think too wildly, as ever I did before I learnt the lesson of calm and composure from the example he set to me.

Now Colonel Brandon goes from Delaford and my calm is quite destroyed! 'My dear Marianne,' said he only this morning – with his horse champing outside on the sweep and he grave and solemn as is the case with him when business matters are concerned, 'My dear child' (Oh how I do hate him looking down the years at me, Elinor: at least your Edward, though he may be weak with it, has his youth still) 'my Marianne, my beloved wife, I go to protect our estates for the sake of our coming child. Can you not comprehend that? Can you not put first the inheritance of our beloved son?'

'Has Dr. Davis told you I shall be delivered of a boy?' said I, very bad-tempered, as you may imagine. 'Then he would have done well to inform the mother also and I will write it to Mama and my dear sister Elinor Ferrars. He must have powers, this Dr. Davis, of which I was unaware.'

At just that time Dr. Davis came in, and heard me; and we had to burst out laughing, from sheer embarrassment.

But not before – and here I ache, as if dear Christopher had raised a fist in anger at me – I heard him murmur, 'I've had enough of daughters to last me a life-time. Now it must be a boy.'

Dearest Elinor, I feel I know to whom Colonel Brandon alludes. He had a love-child, did he not? Why, Mrs. Jennings made much of the fact when we visited her in London and she thought Brandon a good enough match for either of us, despite the love-child, 'prenticed out as she said – or so I heard – for I was ill with weeping then. And this same condition threatens me once more.

Pray tell me, dearest Sister, if you know that there were other children – other daughters indeed – in Colonel Brandon's past life? Is he so utterly sick of fathering daughters that any excuse will have him galloping off at the very mention of a pregnancy? . . . I must be told by return, Elinor – or I shall lose the child, my own life, everything.

Now I shall write to Mama. If you cannot come on the instant then Mama, I know, will not wish her dear Marianne abandoned at such a time. I shall knit – Dr. Davis recommends it strongly, for the nerves. I shall hope, with all the force I can muster, to find you or Mama on the way here; and I must own, if I could have the preference, Elinor, it would be you. For I have another fear – and now Colonel Brandon has left me for Wales, it is to you I must confide it, and straight away.

Is not Colonel Brandon's age against him, when it comes to fathering a child? Are not his advancing years a reason for me to fear my pregnancy? I have a freak within me, Sister, who prefers not to be born and be seen to be the offspring of an old man . . . Oh Elinor, my heart is filled with dread and every possible fear. I write to Mama now: it is not so far from Honiton and she will come post-haste, I know it, though she will scorn my feelings on the subject of Colonel Brandon's age as cause for my having to lie-in seven months, as Dr. Davis very strictly told me I must. 'Why, Colonel Brandon is little more than five years younger than I, Marianne,' Mama will say. 'You will call me old next, I daresay.'

Well I do, indeed I do, Elinor; but Nature has assured that Mama will not bear a child at her time of life; while Colonel Brandon may continue till Doomsday, and bring forth a progeny of monsters, if he so desires.—

I have only one amusing piece to tell you, dear Sister, you must be exhausted by my hysterics by now and I shall seal this and address it to Ferrars Hall in the hope that you are still there, to receive it.

It consists of the following. Dr. Davis, on coming into

the room as I just described to you, heard my mention of my sister Mrs. Ferrars; and he remarked, in the discreetest possible way, that we are very likely connected, if I referred to the Ferrars of Norfolk, at Burnham Overy Staithe. 'My wife, Nancy,' says he – turning all the while to Colonel Brandon as if we were at some social occasion together and I not confined in my night-gown in bed – 'Miss Nancy Steele was my wife's name before we were wed. Her sister Lucy, now Mrs. Robert Ferrars . . . '

For all my apprehensions, reproachful looks at my husband and so forth, Elinor, I could not desist from bursting out laughing. Do you recall, when the Steele sisters ingratiated themselves so very much with Lady Middleton at Barton Park, and then in London, how the elder Miss Steele was laughed at on the subject of a Dr. Davis, who might propose marriage to her, if only he could be brought to the point? How the poor girl was teased! Well, she has him now.— But the idea of her so near in the village, and doubtless dreaming of an invitation to the Mansion-house, filled me with fresh dread, which I was this time forced to pretend came from a sinking or fainting brought about by the child in my womb . . .

I await your reply with feelings which I do not need to reiterate, my dear Elinor. If you do not come I shall believe the worst and think you perished with cold in your empty palace by the sea.

Your affectionate sister,

Marianne

From Elinor Ferrars to John Dashwood

The twenty-sixth of February

Dear Brother,

You will have heard from Mrs. Ferrars of the sad misfortunes which have befallen the family.

We are now removed from Ferrars Hall. The bailiffs came on Friday last, and I regret to say Mrs. Ferrars was only induced to leave after quite a struggle. It did not save her reputation here that creditors were gathered &c., and some mud balls thrown by children of the estate workers, which was most regrettable.

We are at present in an inn that can allow us no more than a two-week stay at most. Edward, from the trust which was so happily set up at the time of his disinheritance by his mother, pays for us all to lodge here; but the sum, as both you and Fanny know, does not add up to a proper competence, and after two weeks have gone by we shall no longer be able to afford the hospitality of the Cock and Bull.

Edward remains here to give comfort to his mother, and

I am here to give him any assistance I can at this very miserable juncture in our lives. It is Edward's duty as a Christian and as a son to care for the parent whose clear preference for Robert, her younger son, was shown but a short time ago. We do not grumble; but it is for a good reason that I must inform you of Robert's departure from Norfolk at the time that the facts of his fraud and bankruptcy were exposed to the world. The consequent difficulties posed for dear Edward, who has a living awaiting him at Delaford, weigh upon us heavily.

Edward feels most strongly that he cannot leave his mother at this time in her life, when all the comforts and style to which she had been accustomed are denied to her. She is no longer sure, I regret to impart to you, of who she is – or where she lodges. Some days she is quite lucid; on others she thinks herself at the Court, in the days of the late King George; or at Park-street, which, like all her other possessions, has been placed under constraint. She accuses me – and this, I may admit to you, dear Brother, is a sore trial to me at times – of taking her jewellery and flaunting it at balls (though which balls she means, in this drear Norfolk landscape where every household keeps to itself in winter – except for hers, that is wide open to the next purchaser in these parts – I cannot say).

All this, as I must explain to you and Fanny, makes harder every day the task of informing Edward's mother that we cannot care for her in perpetuity. Colonel Brandon has shown great generosity to Edward, in offering him the living at Delaford; the Parsonage is in need of repair; and our parishioners must be made to feel welcome to call on us there at the earliest possible opportunity. We have forfeited many of our own personal possessions – which were seized along with those of Mrs. Ferrars, on Friday last: we must buy clothing, and save enough from Edward's income to appear in Dorset clad in something more suitable to the arrival of the new incumbent of the parish than the few articles in which we were forced to flee the park gates.

Even more important than all this, dear Brother, is my strong feeling that all may not be well with my sister Marianne. She writes that she is with child – but that her health is precarious – and she is alone at Delaford, Colonel Brandon having, by necessity, had to go to his estates in Wales. (Even the mail is no longer delivered to Ferrars Hall; and it was only by a stroke of good fortune, as I happened to walk into Burnham, that Mr. Grimmer, who had been accustomed to bring our letters up to the Hall, brought from his bag the latest missive from Marianne, along with creditors' demands addressed to the absent Robert and his mother.) So I feel it imperative that we go to Delaford without delay.

You and Fanny must, I am sure, have considered the housing of Fanny's mother at Norland Park? I can think of no way of asking this of you less bluntly. She speaks of Norland very often, and tells Mrs. Coke, our amiable landlady here, at least ten times a night of the proportions of the house and estate and her relations with it. It is generally expected, by those few neighbours who still have converse with us, that Mrs. Ferrars will go to you directly after the auction of the Hall, in twelve days' time – for she is determined to attend the event, despite warnings from the local medical man that she should not risk going to the Hall in such inclement weather.

In point of fact, Brother, there is a great deal of apprehension in these parts that Mrs. Ferrars may do herself grave injury, should she see the estate go under the hammer here and Mr. Butts the buyer: that she might shout out or otherwise cause herself to be committed to a safe house until after the completion of the sale. Only her removal, *before* the day when all of Norfolk will crowd to the Auction Rooms at King's Lynn, can assure a peaceful and sensible transfer of the Ferrars acres from one hand to another.

Edward and I can only conjecture that his mother, in the confused state in which she finds herself, forgets she is expected daily at Norland Park; that her daughter prepares for her mother's comfort and her son-in-law looks about his park in Sussex to see where he may place a dower house for Mrs. Ferrars that is neither too far from nor too near to the home inherited from our dear father.

We await your reply here. My mother is in good health, I hear from Barton Cottage; and as anxious as we that Edward shall take up his vocation as Parson of Delaford at the soonest possible opportunity.

When we are installed, you are cordially welcomed to come to Delaford; and in the event of ill-health on the part of Marianne I am sure we shall be happy to have you and Fanny at the Parsonage if the Mansion-house is taken up with a confinement and its possible complications.

With affection, dear Brother, and to Fanny,

Elinor

News has just come that Robert Ferrars, who gave no destination at the time of his departure from the Hall, is gone to Africa. His wife – I had not meant to allude to her in a letter which must be read by Fanny – has, it appears, gone to visit her elder sister who was Miss Steele and is married to a Dr. Davis – in our part of the world, it appears, should we ever come to think of Dorset as such a place.

From John Dashwood to Elinor Ferrars

The first of March

My dear Elinor,

It was a pleasure indeed to have news of you, and to be apprised of your dear mother's continuing good health in the salubrious air of Devonshire, where her cousin has so hospitably placed her.

We cannot, alas! do the same for Mrs. Ferrars here in Sussex, and I am astonished – as indeed is dear Fanny – that you have not been informed of this by Mrs. Ferrars herself, to whom we have both written several times over the past weeks.

So – and we must fear that dear Mother's memory has quite gone (for I was not amazed to hear your tales of her wandering mind and confusion as to her place of abode) – I must reiterate to you, Elinor, all the many reasons why it is impossible that Mrs. Ferrars should be lodged here, even for so much as a day.

We are rebuilding the West Wing (did I not inform you of this when we last corresponded, in happier times?) and the mess from the plaster, the continuing presence of the builders and the frequent lack of water, along with other amenities we had all taken for granted since my inheritance of Norland from Papa, have driven poor Fanny almost to despair.

Then the cook, to add to our domestic difficulties, walked from Norland Park a week ago and is not replaced. You may imagine, especially when a young child, our son Harry, is a part of the household, how we are restricted to cold food, put together as best we can (in this freezing weather!) and pray the dirt and dust will not infect his delicate chest, for it flies everywhere.

This work, which is so necessary, is combined with the erection of the Grecian Temple on the hill where the old walnut trees once stood. I do not ask you to consider the expense of such an enterprise, dear Sister – it would not be in your competence to do so. But it drains us to the last farthing: we have cut back on the horses, to pay for the flattening of the knoll and the importing of the statuary – on which dear Fanny doats – from Rome, to complement the Temple. We have dismissed three stable-lads and four chambermaids – though we think the work worthwhile, as there will be a very pleasant view of all the county when once it is done, in however many years the erection of the building will take to complete. 'At least Harry will live to see a better prospect than we have had before him,' says Fanny, who is mindful only of her son and of his future at Norland Park – indeed, I do not believe she would be concerned to hear the West Wing and the Temple were not to be accomplished in her life-time if once she knew our son would reap the benefit of our economies and foresight.

Our worst setback, as it so arises, Elinor, came just a week ago, when rot was discovered in the foundations of the West Wing, and investigations are now in progress to show whether poor Papa's neglect of the house was as widespread as it now appears. We can only pray that we are not, as you are, forced to remove to an inn, with Norland Park absolutely uninhabitable and no date given for our installation here again.

It is therefore our sad duty to inform you that Mrs. Ferrars would find herself a good deal worse off than she is at present, were she foolhardy enough to accept the invitation to live with us for ever that is, I know, engraved on poor Fanny's heart and mine.

And you have put forward a suggestion that we build a dower house. Why, dear Sister, do not you know the expenses the present enclosure of land costs me – and those in my unhappy position? I am stretched enough with that, without thinking of putting up houses all over the place!

We are happy to anticipate our visit to you and the Reverend Edward Ferrars at Delaford and we thank you for the kind invitation. However, when we proposed to visit Marianne in Dorset she informed us almost at once that the winter was very extreme and set in for months of ice and snow there. We are happy to wait until the finer days to come to you at Delaford.

Fanny asks me to convey her sincere affection to you. She is distracted by the builders at this moment, and Harry has fallen and cut his knee on broken glass from the oriel window – we must dress the wound and await the physician – and so I rush with reluctance from this desk and my letter to you.

Your problems, with the aid of Edward's prayer and your own practical nature, will soon be overcome, Elinor. I am certain of it. Just as I believe – indeed, it was Fanny's happy thought – that Robert Ferrars will do splendidly in Africa! He may save the family fortunes yet, dear Sister: for Robert has always doated on ivory, as Fanny reminds me; and was ever particular with his toothpicks, as you may yourself also recall.

We hope to see you in the summer well settled in your Parsonage, though we shall, I expect, be at the Mansion-house with Colonel Brandon and our dear sister Marianne.

Your affectionate brother,

John

BARTON PARK
DEVONSHIRE

From Mrs. Jennings to her daughter
Mrs. Thomas Palmer

The fifth of March

My dear Charlotte,

I trust your nipples are now drawn out and the child sucks, sleeps and thrives. I never did know any woman with such quantities of milk and such difficulty in the giving of it – why, as I remarked to your dear sister yesterday as we returned across the park from a visit to Mrs. Dashwood at Barton Cottage, it was ever thus with the pair of you: what one finds easy to accomplish the other cannot do at all, and vice versa. And it is ever thus with sisters, I daresay, for the Miss Dashwoods come to mind as I write, very likely due to my visit to their mother, now left with just the one, Margaret, who bears more resemblance to Marianne, in my mind, than to Mrs. Edward Ferrars. Yes – the girl has quite an amount of Mrs. Brandon in her and some of the same headstrong nature, as the anecdote I shall now relate to you will show.

But first, how is the weather in London? It cannot be as drear as here, though Sir John professes to like it, for the hunting, and to loathe the frost, as it will spoil his shooting – or is it the other way round? I never can recall, and my memory, as your sister Lady Middleton is quick to inform me, is slipping away as fast as the shillings I spent in Honiton Tuesday last on the purchase of 7 yards bombasine at 6s.6d – a prodigious price, almost as steep as London, when I expected the countryside at the very least to supply me with a bargain.

Whether my memory fades or not, the latest news of the Dashwood family is startling indeed. Mrs. Ferrars has completely forgot who she is – now, Charlotte you cannot say your poor old mother has arrived at that quite yet! – and writes, so I am reliably informed, to the crowned heads of Europe inviting herself to their Courts and then to visit her at Ferrars Hall, which goes under the hammer today – or was it yesterday or next week? – I do not remember which. She is turned against her daughter-in-law Mrs. Edward Ferrars – and, from what I hear, this is not so very surprising, though I did not like to mention any of this to Mrs. Dashwood for fear she would take offence at any imputation against her beloved daughter.

The same Mrs. Edward Ferrars, I am told, has got her hands on all the old lady's jewels – those saved from the creditors and stuffed up a chimney at the Hall, a hiding-place known only to Mrs. Ferrars, her daughter-in-law Elinor and her son Edward. If we are to suspect a parish priest of stealing his mother's gems, things have come to a pretty pass in this country – and I have no doubt Colonel Brandon should be informed of it, before handing over his flock to the tender mercies of a thief. And if it is truly Elinor who is the petty criminal, then that is just as bad.

It appears poor Mrs. Ferrars has only one desire; and that is that she will not be constrained to keep company with Elinor. She sorely misses her son Robert, gone to shoot crocodiles in Mesopotamia, I am told, and she yearns for the company of Robert's wife, Lucy – who was engaged four years to Edward, you know, Charlotte. Mrs. Ferrars moved her assets to Robert, the younger son, when she first heard of Edward's betrothal to Lucy Steele – now she has come to doat on Lucy and Robert has vanished off the face of the earth. It is a strange thing indeed. Very well, I shall confess to you: all the news I am about to impart to you comes in a letter from Lucy herself. She stays with her sister, Nancy Steele, who is now wed to a Dr. Davis and lives in Dorset. 'Oh, it is not so far away,' I said to Mrs. Dashwood at Barton Cottage today; 'Lucy is a splendid young woman. Why do we not all pay a visit to Delaford?' (For that is where they are, dear Daughter, not a stone's throw from the Mansion-house that is now the home of the beautiful young Mrs. Brandon – one of my most successful matches, I often do reflect.) Then, on seeing Mrs. Dashwood's face, I changed the subject entirely – for was not Elinor fortunate to gain the affection of Edward Ferrars, when he had been so long enamoured of Lucy?—What a pretty girl she was! – and still is, I hear. I cannot wait to see her again, for she has a humorous way with her that is markedly different from Elinor's grave comportment: I know which I would prefer as a bride, I can assure you – but here I am, rattling on, when you have the new babe to suckle – do not take too long to wean as you did with Thomas, will you, Daughter? His demanding ways are due to an excessive time at the breast – he kicked me quite severely on the shin when I last came to your new house in Sloane-street – he will wreck all your furnishings if Mr. Palmer does not administer a punishment suitable to his bad behaviour.

No, apart from planning the ball here at Barton Park which Sir John Middleton will give for Margaret, the youngest Dashwood daughter, at Midsummer – what a generous, convivial man he is! – we have little to do here

41

but take short walks; return to the house; sit at tea or dinner; go out again as it grows dark by the stewponds, and prepare ourselves for an evening of cards or basket-weaving. It is dull, I promise you – and if I were not grandmother to Lady Middleton's brood – and poor little Annamaria still laid up in bed since her fall out riding, I would be back in London without the slightest doubt.

The mention of Margaret Dashwood brings to mind my reason for writing you this letter – enquiries after your health and the infant's apart. For you will never believe who I saw, riding on a white stallion just two days ago. It was very misty, so I had to strain my eyes, but there he was, on the crest of the hill and with a young girl running to meet him, arms outstretched. You will not give credence to this, Charlotte. I cannot think how it slipped my mind right at the start of this letter, and now Sir John and the children come in and I am quite interrupted and my writing-table I am sure will be overturned.—

Yes, indeed, I was right to believe that the Middletons' children are as ill-mannered and rough as yours are, Charlotte. My inkbottle was seized and thrown to the ground.—A maid has had to go for ink, and the house so badly managed your sister has come into the room and informed me we shall have to wait until tomorrow for a man to go to Honiton for ink: I continue, as you observe, in a pencil that has been chewed both ends by the dogs . . .

It was John Willoughby I saw on the white horse, Charlotte – can you read this? Your sister still scowls over by the fireplace as if I and not her wretched children had been responsible for the black ink marks on the carpet she had from France by *Aubusson* . . . Can your poor eyes see this scrawl where I tell you that the girl who ran with such joyous abandon towards Willoughby on his white horse, on the hill just above Barton Cottage was Margaret Dashwood herself? How the sight brought back to me the sufferings of poor Marianne, in that summer when her heart was broke and she in my house suffering to the degree that she would not eat my olives, specially procured, or my dried cherries. – And you, dear Charlotte, with your first infant at the breast, had the goodness of heart to put up the Miss Dashwoods at Cleveland, and then had to leave yourself when poor Marianne developed a putrid fever that would be most injurious to a new-born babe . . .

But I ramble. Lord, how this pencil wears to a stump and Sir John, always so ready to oblige, gone out to fish for trout and not here to sharpen it for me. I shall have to end here, Charlotte . . . I heard from your sister just at this very minute that Willoughby's marriage with Miss Grey is accounted a disaster: she has bought herself a great estate somewhere – your sister cannot recall where – and they never see each other. But Mrs. Smith, Willoughby's relation at Allenham, quite forgave him before she died – he is such a rake and a jilt, but he married Miss Grey with fifty thousand pounds and for that anyone would find their sins pardoned. So he has inherited Allenham Court, Mrs. Smith's fine house in Devonshire, having been quite restored to her favour again; he is at Combe Magna, his estate in Somersetshire, and is never visited there by Mrs. Willoughby.

It is strange indeed, when Somersetshire is quite a distance from us here, that Willoughby should choose to ride to Barton Cottage – for that is where he was going, I can promise you.

For all the riches which that young man has now inherited, and a wife who supports herself (and pays for his horses too, so I hear from the groom here), I still am glad in myself that Marianne heeded my excellent advice and married Colonel Brandon. He is so much more of a settled man, he is so kind and devoted – I fear his troubles come from his disappointment in love with his cousin Eliza when he was barely twenty years old: he is slow to respond to any gesture of affection; he is not spontaneous, Charlotte – and though I could agree with you if you were to inform me that Mr. Palmer is not spontaneous either, then at least you find Mr. Palmer excessively droll – which Colonel Brandon decidedly is not.

Now I am reduced to little Annamaria's colours – and I end this missive, my dearest daughter, in a violet paint that will have you believe we are all covered in woad, down in Devonshire. (I must say it is tiresome to have to send three miles for meat, or for ink, for that matter: I cannot think how your sister can endure it.)

We must side with Colonel Brandon.—For I have no doubt that Willoughby, who has never ceased to think of Mrs. Brandon, is gone to Barton Cottage to ingratiate himself with Mrs. Dashwood – to apologise for his treatment of Marianne, I daresay – and to seduce young Margaret into the bargain, if he gets the chance, even though she be but fifteen years old – but as pretty as her sister, and with all the lure of forbidden fruit to a scoundrel such as Willoughby, for she is below the age of consent.—

I shall warn Mrs. Dashwood. If it is fine tomorrow I shall walk over there, and propose a visit to Delaford . . . Then I expect all the story of Willoughby's visit, his wistfulness at the sad fact of his present marriage – caused, I may say, entirely by his own exorbitant level of debt – &c. may come out.—

The groom here also informed me, when I had presented his wife with buns and sat with her a long while in their cottage, that it is well known to all but Mrs. Brandon that the Colonel's love-child and *her* bastard infant are housed on a remote part of the Colonel's Dorsetshire estate.

Poor Marianne . . . just think of it, Charlotte – how *you* would feel if Mr. Palmer had such a ménage tucked away at

Cleveland. You would be indignant, indeed you would be right to be so . . .

Now I swing in the direction of Willoughby and I fancy Marianne would have done better to have married him. Mrs. Smith would very likely have pardoned the lad anyway, for he has charm enough, God knows.

Sir John's groom informed me there is another reason why Mr. Willoughby may ride over in the direction of Eggardon and thereabouts, which is quite the wildest part of the Colonel's Dorsetshire estate.

For Willoughby is the father of the child the Colonel houses there with its poor mother, the Colonel's daughter; yes, Charlotte, it all came out, if you recall, that the reason we could not have the picnic at Whitwell that summer day was that Colonel Brandon was called urgently to London – and it was to attend his daughter who was with child and abandoned by Willoughby.

There is no doubt in my mind that John Willoughby is a very great rake and horribly expensive. But I fear what Marianne may feel when she learns that Colonel Brandon's granddaughter (according to the groom's wife, who is promised a week's supply of sweet pastries if ever I am able to get to Honiton to procure them) is Willoughby's offspring and much visited and doated on by him.

Who would have thought it, Charlotte? Has the scoundrel so mended his ways that he loves a child? What does Colonel Brandon do, if he walks slap into Mr. Willoughby on the occasion of visiting his ward and her infant . . . ?

It is too droll for words. You must not impart any of what follows to a soul, dear Daughter.

For the groom's wife confided in a whisper that Marianne is now with child, though ill with it: she had never the constitution of either of *my* daughters and was much weakened by the fever. It would be injurious to Mrs. Brandon, now the

Colonel has found it necessary to oversee his Welsh estates, if she were to hear of the arrangements he has made for his daughter and her child. And worse still, I tremble to think of it, if she were to learn the name of the visitor who calls so frequently at their humble abode . . .

It occurs to me that Lucy Steele, or Mrs. Robert Ferrars, as I must remember to address her, would in all probability welcome a visit from me at Delaford. Her sister Nancy's husband, Dr. Davis, is physician to the Brandon family: poor Marianne is in his care.

The paint is quite dried out now, and the dogs have climbed up and lapped at the water with which I moistened my brush.—

I send you all my love, dear Charlotte, as do all at Barton Park – and I must add that Miss Margaret Dashwood, who runs between Barton Cottage and the house here like one possessed, shows all the signs of a love-sickness for the scoundrel John Willoughby that her poor sister did, last year – but there are no young men about here to distract her, Charlotte, and it is months until the ball . . .

Your affectionate

Mother

From Elinor Ferrars to Marianne Brandon

The fourth of March 1812

My dear Marianne,

This can be but the briefest return of yours.—There has been much trouble here and Mrs. F. quite out of her mind some days, though clear and lucid on others, and our lives here all the more difficult and strange for that.

Yesterday was the sale of Ferrars Hall, but much to our amazement Edward's mother refused even to hear of the proceedings, electing instead to call out the guards for the reported theft of her jewels, in particular the pearls of Queen Marie-Antoinette – though I have myself much doubt as to the provenance of the necklace, which Mrs. Ferrars prizes above all her other gems.

It was I, sweet sister, who stood accused of purloining the pearls! – I, who have never, as you well can bear witness, worn anything more than Edward's hair – and poor Papa's signet ring that was left me in his will before Fanny claimed it for her own and had Mama return it to the vault at Norland Park.

How could I reply to such an accusation? Can you imagine my shame and humiliation – when, after going up the chimneys at the inn and finding nothing, she had me searched, with Edward helpless to prevent the rough fingers of the guards as they ransacked my dresses and petticoats until I was weeping with mortification?

The oddness of it all, as I say, lies in the fact that Mrs. Ferrars is of occasion amiable to a degree – her mind is not yet totally corrupted ... she will burst forth with intentions to repent and then repeat her vile slanders of me, her daughter-in-law – while calling all the while for her other one, Lucy, who has fled the scene.

I cannot bear it, Marianne; but bear it I must. And all the while I fret over your last letter, my dear: that you are with child is a matter for rejoicing, yet you despond. You lack your adored husband at this time – and I feel your anguish at his absence, of that you may be assured.—But Colonel Brandon would not travel abroad at such a time unless it were imperative for him to save his estates – there is very likely a pestilence among the cattle, or some such, and his delicacy was too great, in your condition, to wish to mention it.

You must not drink too much green tea – you must not excite your imagination, Marianne – for no good can come of frenzy and wild conjecture at this time – think, instead, my sweet Sister, what happiness the birth of your child will bring to you. And do not brood, or hear wrongly when Colonel Brandon speaks of his desire for a son.—Why, Marianne, all men speak thus; even Edward, and he has but two hundred and fifty pounds a year to live on and a sum of ten thousand pounds that will one day be shared among all his progeny. For Mrs. Ferrars did not think of giving more when she welcomed him into the family once more – and now she cannot, though she speaks with bitterness of the vast sum her pearls would raise, had I not swallowed them!

Be of good cheer, my loved one. All the news is good! The weather that is so much to you, even . . . the sun shines for you, Marianne, and you must thank the Lord for your good fortune.

I shall write to Mama – have you done so? I hope she is apprised of the happy event – though doubtless Mrs. Jennings is already in possession of the news if she is at Barton Park, as I assume!

Write to me here. I shall come to Delaford as soon as Mrs. F is settled . . . Edward speaks to the convent at King's Lynn tomorrow and prays the Mother Superior, who has befriended him in past years, will take pity on his mother and give her sanctuary there.

I will confess to you, dear Sister, that my very flesh shrinks at the idea of Edward's mother at the Parsonage. Write to me and tell me I am not heartless, that I do not lack sensibility entirely . . .

By my confession you will understand more fully why I am not already with you at Delaford. We do not speak of the matter, Edward and I, but I know he would not find himself able to carry out his duties if his mother, who has ever been dominant in his life, were to be calling orders night and day. And I – Marianne, am I a monster to turn an old and infirm woman from my door?

But I cannot, even with your own presence to succour me, at the Mansion-house; I cannot—

Mrs. F is brought in, found wandering at Ferrars Hall and accosting Mr. Butts and his family as they strolled in the park they have so recently acquired. We are at our wits' end, Marianne – and still think of your haven of tranquillity and peace as the ultimate goal of our desires . . .

Please do, at the very least, assure me you are reading

prose and not poetry, at this critical juncture in your life. Edward has a fine volume of theosophical teachings which he proposes to send down to you, in the absence of counsel from the estimable Colonel Brandon.

Your affectionate sister,

Elinor

Barton Cottage
Devonshire

From Mrs. Henry Dashwood to Marianne Brandon

The sixth of March

My dear Daughter,

I learnt today – and from Mrs. Jennings at Barton Park – that you expect a child. My loved Daughter, how is it that you have not confided this to me? And now I hear also from that lively old tittle-tattle through Miss Lucy Steele (as was – the sister of the doctor's wife, Mrs. Davis, and it appears gone to Dorsetshire since the collapse of the Ferrars family fortunes) – yes, from as distant a connection as the sister of Mrs. Davis! – that the fact of your pregnancy is well known at Delaford.

Your mother alone was not apprised of this momentous news, Marianne.

What can this forebode? That you are discontented, with so kind and devoted a husband as Colonel Brandon – why, it is scarcely conceivable!

It was no more than two weeks ago that Colonel Brandon wrote to me himself and spoke of all the measures he has taken in the winter cold to wrap you up and keep you warm and out of danger – for your chest will never recover fully, after the fever you suffered at Cleveland, Marianne – and no-one is more concerned than dear Christopher that you shall not succumb to pneumonia, or pleurisy, or another bout of the putrid illness that nearly took you from us, beloved angel.

Colonel Brandon wrote to me of the mustard baths and flannel petticoats he has provided for you at Delaford. Can you not feel for him the love and gratitude that he deserves from you? Are you, my dear child, brooding as you were wont to do?—Why, you have more good books to read than when you were just a maid and in thrall to *The Mysteries of Udolpho* and to tales of animated puppets and ghosts that walked the earth at cock's crow – and all manner of spectral things!

You are educated now, dear Daughter, and all at the behest of Colonel Brandon – who has gone as far as any man could in procuring knowledge for his young wife.— Why, even the subject of mathematics has been introduced to you, Marianne – you are not ever with your nose in romances and poetry.—My child, you have so much to thank Colonel Brandon for . . .

Now there is a carriage out on the road and it stops. Oh, it will be Sir John. He is as promiscuous with his invitations to Barton Park as ever, and I must confide I do on occasion miss a time to sit sewing quietly, as there is always one entertainment or other up at Barton Park.— Yes. Sir John enters. I lay down my pen . . .
(*letter interrupted*)

119 Sloane-street
London

From Mrs. Thomas Palmer to Mrs. Jennings

The sixth of March

Dear Mother,

In receipt of your letter – Lord, it sounds dull at Barton
Park – how you can bear the company of my sister's children
and none other (for Sir John cannot be counted as a grown
man; he is as boisterous as a child) I cannot imagine—

My babe is well, and Mr. Palmer so droll when he came
from his club last night and professed himself astonished
to find an infant here.—'Why, Charlotte, are you already
delivered?' said he. 'I had clean forgot!' Then the good man,
sitting himself down on the bed, proceeded to inform me that
Lady Lumpton had suffered the preceding night the return
of his lordship, who, being much in liquor, entered the
bedchamber and sat down full on her face whilst removing
his boots. The good lady could merely struggle and groan
and he too full of wine to attend her remonstrances. Was
that not droll, Mama? La! How I laughed.

London is cold and grey and we think we may come to you
at Easter for all that there is no amusing company at Barton

Park. The place was tolerable when the Miss Steeles spent time there, and they had some use in taking the children out to play; but we shall come, nevertheless. I expect Lucy will come and be with us there. Sir John does not care how many he has in the house; and Lucy writes to me that her cards left at the Mansion-house at Delaford have not been returned. Mrs. Brandon has taken on airs at a fine speed, has she not, Mother?—for it is well known that Colonel Brandon married her from pity of her condition after she made public an engagement that did not exist. It is a lesson to a young girl, to keep the state of her heart discreet – and it is no secret either that Mrs. Brandon rewards her husband by yawning in his face and going out, long after all the household is abed, to stand in the moonlight by the turnpike road . . .

I have little to impart to you at a time of year when all but the most intrepid hostess keeps to her house alone and issues no invitations: Spring has not yet come, it is as dark as winter, but without the balls. But, on the topic of the Brandons, I will impart one choice morsel.

In Bond-street, just three days ago, I was fatigued from attending the babe hours on end and the nurse so dozy I dared not leave her alone with him, so I went out walking, despite the constant drizzle and the unfamiliar faces of women in dresses that were far from modish – where do they appear from, at this time of year? – when I perceived a couple walking in the Arcade and talking in an animated fashion.

My dear Mother, I confess I found myself gawping like any tripper at the sight of Colonel Brandon – yes, he it was! – in company with a young woman. They had come from the Academy: I heard them speak of Sir Joshua Reynolds . . . She wore a fine cape that looked new and was trimmed with fur that could have been rabbit but I do believe was ermine – *Someone* had lavished a very great deal of money on the

young lady, in short, and very recently – I have writ all
this to Lucy to enquire if she knows who the Colonel's
companion can be . . .

Mr. Palmer is just in and calling for mulled wine to
counter-act the miserable cold he caught shooting at Lord
Lumpton's last week, so I must fetch it – the servants here
are every one of them quite deaf.

My most sincere regards to Sir John and to his wife, my
dear sister

Your daughter,

Charlotte

*Resumed letter from Mrs. Henry Dashwood to
Marianne Brandon*

The sixth of March

<u>Evening</u>

My dear child, forgive this lapse of time – but I was
caught quite unawares I must confess, by the arrival of a
visitor. The carriage to which I alluded was not Sir John
from Barton Park – and now I repent my spoilt complaint
of his taking up my time with suppers and dancing at the
House, when already such a time appears a lost Eden, a
Paradise to which I strive to return.

The barouche brought none other than Mrs. Ferrars
to Barton Cottage, Marianne. She climbed down, eyes

57

glittering in a most terrifying manner and her dress torn to shreds as if she had been in combat (as she then proceeded to inform me had indeed been the case, for it appears the carriage is no longer hers, and the present owner, at Ferrars Hall in Norfolk, had remonstrated violently with her). She had bribed the coachman with money from Elinor's house-keeping – so she boasted.

Oh Marianne, poor Elinor! As so often in past years I have given all my love and commiseration to one daughter – to you, my sweet child – and I have not considered Elinor and her heart's sorrows. For her feelings run just as deep as yours, as we are both of us aware, but for *her* it is difficult to give utterance to them, whereas, with *you*, dear Daughter, the slightest cold in the head becomes a drama worthy of the great William Shakespeare. (I sense I offend you – I do not have that intention, Marianne. Please believe me.)

Mrs. Ferrars first embarked on her visit to me by demanding I 'give back' the plate, linen and china I had 'stolen' from Norland Park at the time of our coming here to Barton Cottage.

I was unable to reply to her: I trembled in every joint, as if the ague had come in the door and seized me . . . I cried to our Thomas here to go fetch Sir John immediately . . .

Mrs. Ferrars, when her ranting and raving were done, fell asleep as suddenly as she had threatened me; and Jane and Mary together carried her to your room – or the room I still think of as yours, my precious child. She lies there now – her snores rattle the window-panes of the cottage.

Oh, why do not Fanny and John do something for Mrs. Ferrars? She is after all Fanny's mother. I am unable to write more as I hear a carriage on the road and pray this time that it *is* Sir John Middleton, come from Barton Park on receipt of Thomas's message. If at least he is not out – but no, this is not the season to shoot duck—

(*letter interrupted*)

From Mrs. Robert Ferrars to Mrs. Brandon

The sixth of March

Dear Mrs. Brandon,

I pray you will forgive an imposition on your valuable time from one who suffers, as do I and your poor sister Elinor, from the recent misfortunes of the Ferrars family. We are an outcast tribe indeed, and were it not for the Christian virtues which will, I know, bring Edward solace in the coming years, we would find ourselves 'wandering in the desert' and without so much as a roof over our heads.

As it is, my sister Nancy, married, as I am sure you are aware, to kind Dr. Davis of this village, has offered her poor sister shelter, until such time as the cottage on the Delaford estate is built that will house Mrs. Ferrars and myself, a daughter-in-law as devoted now in her hour of tribulation as ever in the days of grandeur, Park-street, Ferrars Hall &c. For I am not one to judge a person by his worldly goods; Mrs. Ferrars is as dear to me without a stick of furniture to her name as when she was vastly rich (and, in any case, I am informed that your mother Mrs. Dashwood intends to return the plate, linen and china wrongly removed from Norland Park) – and that this, with all the generosity for which dear Fanny is known throughout the county of Sussex, will in turn be lent to Mrs. Ferrars to assist with the furnishing of the cottage built at Delaford by Colonel Brandon.

I would have written to you before, dear Neighbour, if I had not been under the impression there was no-one at the Mansion-house at present. My cards have not been returned; and – a more compelling reason to consider you must be abroad – my friend Mrs. Palmer informed me she saw both Colonel Brandon and yourself in Bond-street just a week ago. She was mistaken, I must suppose; though the distinguished Colonel Brandon is surely easy enough to pick out in a crowd.

Now, I am delighted to see you must both have returned, doubtless from a trip to buy clothes for the infant – a joyous day awaits you, dear Mrs. Brandon, and the fact that your sister will be brought to bed first – is her child not due at Midsummer? – will of course in no way detract from the very great pleasure of the event. Dr. Davis will attend you both, I daresay – for Mrs. Edward Ferrars will by all accounts be well settled in the Parsonage by then.

If you are in communication with your sister Elinor, can you discover when she expects to settle here at Delaford? Several of the parishioners are most anxious to meet their new rector; and one in particular, Mrs. Cox, has heard of the misfortunes of my mother-in-law Mrs. Ferrars and knits for her: so far a pair of socks, which I think will prove extremely beneficial in the cold weather, do not you agree?

Many of the other Christian souls in this fine village also wish to extend their hospitality and compassion to Mrs. Ferrars in her hour of need; and daily expect her at the Parsonage, where she will surely abide until the completion of the cottage.

On which subject, I beg you, Mrs. Brandon, to permit me to enclose the very fine scale drawing made by my husband Robert before his departure to Africa in order to harness the great waterfalls in the provision of power to drive the mills of the simple natives there. (He has already investors in the scheme; the name of Ferrars is not done with yet.)

The plan shows the maximum use of space for the cottage – it can hold as many as eighteen couples, should the parlour be proportioned as Robert has designed it. He hoped Colonel Brandon would find his proposals of use when consulting his architect.

I shall take the liberty of calling on you again, Marianne – may I? – and shall hope to find you at home.

Yours faithfully,

Lucy Ferrars

Barton Cottage
Devonshire

*Resumed letter from Mrs. Henry Dashwood to
Marianne Brandon*

The seventh of March

O my dear child, what a night we have had!

All the confusion that came in the train of the arrival of
Mrs. Ferrars made the hours pass as if they were but seconds.
It was Jane – no, it was Mary – I do not recall which of the
maids – who was the first to see that your sister Margaret
was not at home . . . There had been neither sight nor sound
of her since morning, as far as anyone knew (for we were
all in a spin), and even as we attempted to remember when
we had last seen the poor girl, all gave differing accounts of
glimpsing her: Thomas espied her in the park, heading for a
game of cards with Lady Middleton, and he was positively

sure she had told him that; Mary saw poor Margaret out at the washing-line at the end of the orchard, where she had left a book the day before; and I myself, who recalled suddenly and with a dreadful jolt of fear, that she had announced she would walk on the hills behind Barton Park.

I told her it would rain and she said it would not; it was true the sky was blue at the time of speaking, but persons of her age cannot see one moment into the future: they will not see a puddle of rain for fear it may prevent their sport; and so it is that they go out in inclement weather quite unprotected and come down a day or so later with an influenza or some other dangerous infection. You, dear Marianne, did not *you* expose yourself to the climate? – and to the fluctuations of your own soul also – and you were so very ill . . .

Foolish girl – and it is of Margaret I speak now, not of the wise and calm Colonel's wife, who has more sense, thank goodness, nowadays, and has no longer the sensibility of past times.

God is to be thanked once again, for your prudent and happy marriage to Colonel Brandon.

I write – I run on – because, as must be clear to the daughter of so worrisome and devoted a mother as your own, Margaret did return from her walk: but only at past eleven o'clock; she was soaked to the skin; all our search parties had proved fruitless, on the great hill that rises above Barton Park.

We were all distraught here. Mrs. Jennings and Lady Middleton came down from the House and sat with me – and this was kind but was also a difficulty, in so small a cottage, for they were intrigued to know the source of the great snores that emanated from the room at the top of the stairs. I held back, I confess, from telling all, in case Elinor might suffer were it known her mother-in-law lay there comatose: then the truth had to come out, as ever it will, for Mary entered and asked if Mrs. Ferrars should be taken up a bowl of soup, and there was talk of fetching physicians and the rest – when, as I grieve to admit, I thought only of Margaret, and saw her each minute with a sprained ankle, stumbling on a precipice or in a wood, as once befell you, Marianne . . .

As chance would have it, Mrs. Ferrars woke just as the dear girl, who came in like a somnambulist, found her way back to the cottage.

Without looking to the right or the left, Margaret made her way up the stairs (I cannot think what Lady Middleton and her mother can make of it all – it was as if we were sworn enemies, Margaret and I, when we are forever, as you well know, embracing each other and want only your company and that of Elinor to find complete happiness at Barton Cottage).

Well, chance dictated that Mrs. Ferrars woke at that instant and shouted some word.—As you are full-grown now, Marianne, I would confide it to you, but for the fear my letter may once more be interrupted, and read, if not with the explicit intention, by Jane or Mary – or, which would be worse still, Thomas.

Margaret screamed – she ran to the door of the room kept in preparation for you, Marianne, and adorned with all the sweet mementoes of your youth – and she fell down in amazement and horror at what met her gaze within those dear, sweet, safe walls, my child.

Mrs. Ferrars – Oh, a horrid old woman – Margaret thought her a witch and cried out words to that effect – Mrs. Ferrars seized a broom and beat the poor child about the head, calling her a thief and an intruder. In the end, as Mrs. Jennings had truly said, there was no choice but to call the physician, who came out three miles from Honiton and administered laudanum.

We were none of us abed until three, dear Daughter. Please forgive the incoherence of my words to you – and my lack of sympathy and understanding of your feeling solitary and dull at Delaford . . .

I would rather a hundred times be with you behind those quiet stone walls, than in the inferno of Barton Cottage at present, Marianne. Rest assured that yours is the more blessed of the two domiciles . . . and Mrs. Ferrars, who talks wildly of visiting you and of the Colonel constructing a 'magnificent cottage' for her in the grounds of Delaford, has been invited to dinner at Barton Park tomorrow, to take her mind from the subject. How kind Mrs. Jennings is – for it was her idea and her daughter is ever slow to follow behind . . .

Midday

I was about to hand the letter to Mary, to catch the Express, when – Oh Marianne I am fortunate indeed! – there came the sound of another carriage on the road beyond the hedge. We all ran out, for Mrs. Ferrars's presence in the cottage will make any excuse worth going outside, despite the constant rain – and there, to my vast and inexpressible relief, were Elinor and Edward.

They had come post-haste overnight. Edward had found his mother gone from the inn where all were lodged at this disastrous juncture in the fortunes of the Ferrars family.

He wasted an hour or more searching Ferrars Hall, where no-one had seen her, just on that day, though she had been there constantly to plague and molest poor Mr. and Mrs. Butts. (Edward did not phrase it in this manner, dear Marianne, but I guessed his meaning.) And so my dear Elinor and her husband came rushing here. For Elinor had heard her mother-in-law had the intention of stealing my plate and linen and china. Of this I cannot write without feeling a flush of fever mount to the cheek. I thank Elinor for having kept until now the desires of Fanny Dashwood and her mother from me – but I do not know I can look John – my own stepson! – in the eye since this.—

But now the letter must go to you. By God's mercy, my Elinor is here. Edward will surely find a sanctuary for Mrs. Ferrars and we shall all be calm once more.

We are now all invited to Barton Park for dinner tomorrow, though I cannot say I anticipate the event with anything other than the utmost dread. With Mrs. Ferrars they do not know what they have invited up to the House.

But I have Elinor and Edward; and Margaret, the good Lord be thanked, is healthy and in excellent spirits: as if her walk in the white mist that came down on the high hill, with all the accompanying rain and bluster, had proved beneficial rather than the contrary.

Margaret says she will not come to Barton Park tomorrow evening. I cannot think why not – but, as you will remember, Marianne, 'tis a strange time of youth when the beauty of maidenhood bursts forth, and there is no accounting for the mood of the day or hour.

Margaret says she learns sonnets to recite on the next occasion of a gathering at Barton Park. And, strange though it may be to admit, I do believe her, for all the lack of interest in poetry the child has yet shown.

I trust you will ask Colonel Brandon, as soon as he is at Delaford once again, to set up a programme of instruction for Margaret that will be as beneficial to her character and intellect as the learning and advice he has imparted to you, his dear wife, Marianne.

Your affectionate

Mother

Meg's Dwelling
Delaford

From Mrs. Meg Cox to Miss Margaret Dashwood

The seventh of March

(Conveyed by Betsy Hands to her sister Jane Hands, servant at Barton Cottage. Receipt as requested.)

To bring fond return of love:

Pound together in the mortar pomegranate seeds, orange and dried lavender of yesteryear. Add wine of the sweet grape of a southern clime; apply to the region of the breast wherein lies the heart and rub with soft moss, gathered from the heights of Barton Tor. The one you love will think of you tonight.

Meg of Delaford

Delaford House
Dorsetshire

From Marianne Brandon to Elinor Ferrars

The seventh of March

My dear Sister,

I learn from Mama that you are come to Devonshire. Oh that you had come here instead! – though Mama would be cruelly stranded without you at Barton Cottage, it is true, and I must come to understand that I am alone in the world; that no-one loves me and I am without family or husband, sweet caress or embrace of a sister's love.

I married a man incapable of feeling, Elinor: a man old enough to be my father but eager enough in his attentions to other women to fancy himself a lover still: a vain coxcomb who parades as tutor, loving spouse and comrade to his wife

– oh, my dear Sister, that I should be the wife of such a man as Colonel Brandon!

For the wretch is seen walking in London with another – yes, a young woman who hangs on his every word as I was pleased to do: a wretch in a fur-trimmed cape who learns of Plato and the philosophers – as if the knowledge she thus gleans will do her good, when she discovers herself in the presence of an adulterer . . .

I am betrayed, dear Elinor. I had no love for Brandon in the first place, as you well know: my health was much deteriorated by the putrid fever suffered by reason of the ill-treatment of another; and the expectations of Mama and yourself for my marriage to Colonel Brandon were such that I could not find the strength in me to resist them.

Now I repent at leisure. So the old saying is true – I am to pass my life in this dull prison; the walls that hold me here bind me to an old man, whose child I must bear in patience, gratitude and silence. I am the unluckiest woman alive, Sister, and even you cannot save me from my fate.

For I see now with a clarity denied to women blinded by the lace and lovebirds – all the sweet nonsense that covers over the reality of pain and sacrifice – that the lot of all women is mine; that married love is very likely a pretence; and that the most foul hypocrisy attends women's lives and trajectories in this harsh world.

We are no more than beasts, Elinor: we are in the world to bear children and tolerate neglect and indifference: if we try to escape our slavery we are beaten by starvation and poverty into obedience; we are chattels indeed and do not own so much as our names, our children or the homes we are encouraged to prettify and grace with our fair smiles.

We have no redress, in the face of this monstrous injustice. We cannot go to law when we are treated brutally; we cannot but survive or die.

I would gladly choose the latter, save that I bear a child and cannot bring myself to destroy another life with mine.

So I shall pace within the walls of Delaford without love or hope; I shall grow old here and pass unmourned to the grave.

To make matters worse still, dear Sister, the horrid Lucy Ferrars invites herself up to the house for tea! Your enemy, Elinor, is ensconced here, I am sorry to say, and her sister's husband, Dr. Davis, will attend me in my confinement. It gives me little pleasure to imagine Mrs. Davis and her sister apprised of every detail of my lying-in – and passing on the information, I have no doubt, to the young companion of Colonel Brandon. For it was Lucy who apprised me in a letter that Mrs. Palmer had seen them together in Bond-street. They had come from the Academy. I am not permitted to go to London and look at pictures; I am no more than Mrs. Brandon now.

My hand shakes and I sob as I pen this to you, dear Elinor. I feel my selfishness – for your life with Mrs. Ferrars is beyond anything. I have not even spoken on the subject of your pregnancy – how could you withhold it from me, Elinor?

Poor Mama! Oh she will give John and Fanny a piece of her mind and it surprises me only that she has not done so before.

But I think only of the unhappy fate of your affectionate sister,

Marianne

From John Willoughby to Marianne Brandon

The seventh of March

My dear Mrs. Brandon,

You will recall perchance that a gift of a horse was once made to you – a fine horse for a woman to ride – since your esteemed mother was not able to provide a mount for you at the time.

My dear, my very dearest Marianne, my groom brings Queen Mab to you today.

Just as I said – and the words are etched on my mind in perpetuity – Queen Mab will one day receive you. But this time you are to receive *her* – dare I hope she will bring you back to me?

Marianne, I have watched you from afar, but I have not had the heart, the courage—

I have not forgot you, my dearest love. No woman has ever or will ever measure up to you. I have always retained that decided regard which interests me in everything that befalls you. You are my secret standard of perfection in a woman – and many a rising beauty has found herself slighted by John

Willoughby, as bearing no comparison with Mrs. Brandon.

> Being your slave, what should I do but tend
> Upon the hours and times of your desire?
> I have no precious time at all to spend,
> Nor services to do, till you require.
> Whilst I, my sovereign, watch the clock for you,
> Nor think the bitterness of absence sour
> When you have bid your servant once adieu;
> Nor dare I question with my jealous thought
> Where you may be, or your affairs suppose,
> But, like a sad slave, stay and think of nought
> Save, where you are how happy you make those.
>> So true a fool is love that in your will
>> Though you do any thing, he thinks no ill.

Walk to your window, loveliest Marianne; look out and behold Queen Mab. I bred the mare myself on my estate here: she is exactly calculated to carry a woman.

Come to me, my dearest. Forget that cruel fate caused Willoughby to be the one to say adieu.

Life cannot be a prison, Marianne. For such as you and I there must be no anchors, but instead the freedom of a bird, a lark that flies high, regardless of the drear world that lies beneath.

Now Allenham is mine – but come to me first here at Combe Magna, where a design for a new future awaits the sweet approval of your smile. Come to me, my beloved – Queen Mab will bring you safely here.

John Willoughby

From Mrs. Henry Dashwood to Lady Middleton

The eighth of March

My dear Lady Middleton,

I write to express my thanks at your very great hospitality and tolerance on the occasion of our family party accepting your distinguished invitation to dinner at Barton Park; that I must tender the most profuse apologies along with my sincere appreciation of the delicious food, the fine company and the atmosphere of discreet pleasure always provided at your house is unfortunate, but alas! – I find it is necessary.

I must confess, dear Lady Middleton, that I had had no notion before her unexpected arrival at Barton Cottage of the extent of the distress to poor Mrs. Ferrars that her recent misfortunes have wrought.

I did not anticipate that she would use your dining-table as she did (I will make no future reference to the despoliation of so magnificent a repast) or that the remainder of the evening would be dominated by her musical efforts. I am only relieved her son Edward was present, to escort her back to our cottage, and that Admiral and Mrs. Flowers, whom you were kind enough to invite to meet us, did not complain too vigorously at Mrs. Ferrars's remarks on the subject of our brave men who fight for England at sea.

I am due to apologise most sincerely, also, for the appearance – and then absence – of my youngest daughter, Margaret. Both your mother, the delightful Mrs. Jennings, and yourself, have unfailingly shown kindness to my daughters; Marianne and Margaret are perhaps not so unalike, in their impulsive natures and their love of poetry – though I confess this latter obsession has grown with Margaret at an alarming rate in recent days.

So I felt myself able to count on your continuing toleration of behaviour that would by most hostesses be considered ill-mannered in the extreme, viz. Margaret's refusal of an invitation to dinner at Barton Park, followed by her sudden arrival when dinner had already commenced and the guests were seated at table; and her subsequent flight out into the park, despite the Spring rain, to run barefoot – as she terms it – amongst daffodils that come before the swallow dares.

That Margaret is now confined to bed at Barton Park after stumbling and falling in a badger burrow or rabbit hole in the dark causes me even greater embarrassment. Dear Lady Middleton, if the child had not contracted a violent head cold alongside her twisted ankle I would insist that Edward, with the aid of our man, Thomas, come to the House to fetch her home now. But after our very dreadful experiences with Marianne at Cleveland, I do not dare to suggest moving the patient at this time.

Elinor has asked me to remind you that the physician must present his fees to us, here; and that you are not to be troubled with sending three miles for any physic that may be required. One of us can go into Honiton at any hour of the day, providing there are two persons remaining here to distrain Mrs. Ferrars, should she wake and fancy herself elsewhere.

I hope and trust that, at the apposite time, you and Sir John will accept a return of hospitality at Barton Cottage. A day cannot at present unfortunately be determined, for reasons too painful to delineate here.

With very sincere gratitude and repeated apologies, dear Lady Middleton

Yours faithfully,

Mary Dashwood

From Elinor Ferrars to Marianne Brandon

The eighth of March

My dear Sister,

I am most distressed to receive your letter. I am sure you do Colonel Brandon an injustice. It is strange indeed that he should be seen in Bond-street in London; but rumour and malice dwell forever at the roots of our society, dearest Marianne, and it is due to the purity of your heart that you do not know this yet. The likelihood is that Lucy has some motive for attracting attention to her presence in Delaford, and manufactures the story, half-heard from Mrs. Palmer. I am most agitated on your behalf but cannot think of any other explanation. Be of good cheer, Sister: Colonel Brandon loves you, and you him; even if you doubt it at times, the sanctity of the marriage vows cannot be betrayed.

Marriage is an act of choice, Marianne. You chose Colonel

Brandon and he you, and you are man and wife in the eyes of the Lord. Edward joins me in praying for the recovery of your mind and spirit, that you may bring a healthy infant into the world at the appointed time.

Oh, my beloved Sister, what a pompous prig my words do make me sound!

But this is a testing time for you: it is true that I do wish your husband at your side now and not far from you; and please believe my reason for keeping my own happy secret from you was purely on account of wishing you calm and serene, and knowing my news would bring you racing to my side – which, at this time in your pregnancy, would not be wise.

Nor would I wish you with us at present, for all that Mama and I talk of you and dream of you night and day.— You would find Mrs. Ferrars an intolerable strain on your nerves. And, as I must impart to you – for otherwise you will hear of it through our maid Jane Hands's sister Betsy at Delaford – Margaret took a bad tumble last night at Barton Park and has a head cold as a complication, which keeps her up at the House and not, as dear Mama and I would wish, with us here at Barton Cottage. (Though chances of her recovery while in the cramped quarters this house provides, with Mrs. F. in residence, would be slim indeed.)

I am called by Edward to assist with his mother, who wishes to call on Lady Middleton again and is not invited there, though she claims Sir John has instructed her to think of his house as her home.

Dear Sister, write to me by return, I pray you. We are so concerned for you, and we send all our fondest love

Your affectionate sister,

Elinor

BARTON PARK
DEVONSHIRE

From Mrs. Jennings to Mrs. Thomas Palmer

The ninth of March

My dear Daughter,

The weather here remains drear in the extreme.—No leaves on the trees; the sun quite gone behind the hill as if it were Christmas Day; and my precious daffodils trampled by the youngest Dashwood girl, who ran out into the rain last night, and, it being pitch dark, twisted her ankle into the bargain.

Margaret is laid up here. It quite takes me back to poor Marianne when she was sick with the putrid fever at Cleveland. Is Mrs. Dashwood the only person in the vicinity not to know her daughter is love-sick? Poor Mrs. Dashwood! Margaret moans of the Wild West Wind or some such thing. She has had her head filled with nonsense.—But, all the more unpersuadable that she has taken leave of her senses by virtue of the charms of her seducer. Oh dear, I do not know what I can do with the child. She asks for a compress of moss from Barton Tor, she threatens to come down with the fever as bad as her sister Marianne . . . Such young men should be banned from Society.

85

I send my love and kisses to the infant. Do you name it yet? In the case of a girl there is never so much of a hurry, for who can say how she will end up by way of nomenclature, and I am sure I would not have imagined a daughter of mine as Charlotte Palmer and would have made my choice a Polly or a Prudence had I known.

The sole amusement we have had here was the dinner last night attended by Mrs. Dashwood's party. Admiral and Mrs. Flowers were present, but were as dull as ever; poor Elinor is a good deal older in the face, and has quite lost her bloom, though when she is delivered of her child she may improve in looks again; Edward Ferrars is still a sad and sorry figure, as I have always found him; and Mrs. Dashwood is herself a bundle of nerves but making an effort almost too remarkable to show conviviality in the face of the family misfortunes which have befallen Edward and his mother.

Of whom, dear Charlotte, we received the most entertaining evening we have known for many a month at Barton Park.

The old lady fairly sparkles; Sir John was beside himself with laughter and promised that if Margaret did not recover her spirits by Midsummer he would give the ball for Mrs. Ferrars instead!—and your sister was vastly amused by the anecdotes, some quite without discretion and tact, which poured from Mrs. Ferrars without restraint.

It was quite a show, dear Daughter, I wish you could have seen the fine dance – a *fandango* or *flamenco*, or some such, as Mrs. Ferrars informed us – which she performed after dinner upon the dining-table, and all our usual reserve quite swept away by her charms and prowess at the Spanish dance steps – though Mrs. Dashwood was most downcast and Edward and Elinor unable to look at each other or at his mother for the duration of it. Your husband, Charlotte, would have found the performance immensely droll, and you would, also, I am convinced of it.

Otherwise I am able only to report that the gamekeeper's brother at Delaford was here with plovers' eggs (which I placed in a fine nest in the centre of the table, and this was much admired) and as he walked back along the park to the road I asked him intelligence of Colonel Brandon's love-child, the daughter so scandalously seduced by our local – and universal – villain, Willoughby, and purported to be hidden away somewhere, as you are aware, on the Colonel's Dorsetshire estate.

'Oh no, Madam,' says he, and with a look of great surprise so I knew he answered the truth. And he proceeded to inform me that Colonel Brandon had took his daughter to London with him to fit her out with dresses and to enjoy the company of some young people she had known before she went to Bath and fell into that scoundrel's clutches (the good man did not phrase it thus, but 'twas what he intended). The child that resulted from this disgraceful encounter is gone to Wales with its nurse; and after the short season Colonel Brandon gives the poor girl in London, she will join her bastard offspring there and live in obscurity, on the Welsh borders where Colonel Brandon has his estates.—And the man added there was fine partridge to be got there, and salmon bursting the banks of the river – though, to my mind, this plenty will be scant recompense to a mother of seventeen years and her babe.

Colonel Brandon must have done all this from delicacy, Charlotte – do not you agree? – his love for Marianne being so great he would not have her stumble across the traces of his past, while on his land at Delaford. I admire and respect the man for this: he is a good father, and as much of a father to Marianne his wife, as to his own daughter, I do not doubt.

Now I see a strange sight from my window. Mrs. Ferrars runs up the steps. She is pulled back by Edward; then Sir John comes out, laughing hugely. Now they are all set off in the direction of the dovecote, for the rain has eased, if even for a short while.

Margaret calls for me, my pet, and I must go. There is no end to maternity, even if I stand in only as replacement for poor Mrs. Dashwood, as you will be sorry one day to discover.

Your affectionate

Mother

From Marianne Brandon to Elinor Ferrars

The eleventh of March

My dear Sister,

I cannot thank you for yours. But I shall forgive you, from the deep happiness of my heart.

My life has heretofore been without meaning or direction. I have been harnessed to a man more than twice my years, a man whose rheumatism increases in the Dorsetshire winter, who wears a flannel waistcoat now almost every day of the week; and who leaves to disport himself in London in preference to keeping the company of his pregnant wife.

But no longer, Elinor! I did not marry for love; nor did he believe I did.

Never have I been so fully aware that we have one life –

before we are translated to that ground beneath the realm of Pluto where all men and all things shall be as one . . . Never have I felt, in all my senses and my being, so alive!

Love is inevitably consequent upon the perception of loveliness. Love withers under constraint; its very essence is liberty; it is compatible with neither obedience, jealousy nor fear; it is there most pure, perfect and unlimited, where its votaries live in confidence, equality and unreserve.

No, Elinor, these are not the teachings of the old man who purports to be my husband but is instead a father and an ancient *philosophe*, a man who would teach me the meek comportment and expectations of the women of an age long gone.

I am in love, Elinor!—I have a new horse, a beauty, and I ride as far afield as Somersetshire. I tell you this solely for reason of that indissoluble bond – whatever your disapproval of my actions may be – which will always exist between us.

I demand that you leave me the liberty of thought and action which are the Rights of Woman – Woman who has been for so many centuries wronged by men and by Society.

Now Queen Mab is at the door. Adieu, dear Sister.

Marianne

From John Willoughby to Marianne Brandon

The twelfth of March

My Beloved,

Now you have made me happy, my sweetest love, no words save those of poetry can express my joy at our mutual tenderness, our freedom, our ecstatic union.

For if I have freed you from patriarchal tyranny, you, Marianne, have brought to me the supreme gift: the gift of your being; you are my other self, and just as you are a half of Willoughby, so Willoughby is the so fortunate other side of the heavenly orb that is Marianne.

That orbèd maiden with white fire laden
Whom mortals call the Moon
Glides glimmering o'er my fleece-like floor,
By the midnight breezes strewn;
And wherever the beat of her unseen feet,
Which only the angels hear,
May have broken the woof of my tent's thin roof,

The stars peep behind her and peer;
And I laugh to see them whirl and flee,
Like a swarm of golden bees,
When I widen the rent in my wind-built tent,
Till the calm rivers, lakes and seas,
Like the strips of the sky fallen through me on high,
Are each paved with the moon and these.

You are the moon to my sun, Marianne, and together, from our wind-built tent, we shall build ourselves a commune where all are equal beneath our rays; where all men are brothers; where none shall go in want and there shall be neither greed nor grief.

My adored Marianne – for many years I have dreamt of Coleridge's ideal society – and it is not solely his, for the Pantisocratic colony that was envisaged by him and Robert Southey came to my mind before I even heard of it from others – but you do not know these names, and a moon-goddess has no need of them. Let me say, then, that for long I have prayed that one day we would go there together, you and I, to the country which is as close to your perfection as your own mirror image, my beloved Marianne.

That country is in the New World.

On the banks of the Susquehannah we shall set up our tents. All peace-loving followers of freedom and equality will follow us there, Marianne. All children will be reared as equal, of whichever sex; the tyranny of the monotheistic god will not touch us there; in our Platonic ecstasy we shall be one with soil and water, fire and sun.

Come to me, Marianne. We shall leave Combe Magna together and embark from Plymouth when the Equinoctial March gales are done and fair April welcomes Marianne's pale head—

I have hired a boat, for Mrs. Smith left me rich and I no

longer suffer the unpleasant necessity of living at another's expense.

We shall need no money in the New World. The fruits of our labours will be reward enough: to each man according to his needs, in that land rich in myth and magic, far from the cruelty of the oppressive God.

I come for you, Marianne. Await me – and prepare yourself—

Your

Willoughby

The Old Rectory
Delaford

From Mrs. Percy Roberts to Elinor Ferrars

The twelfth of March

Dear Mrs. Ferrars,

I obtained your mother Mrs. Dashwood's address at Barton Cottage from Mrs. Jenkins, housekeeper at Delaford Manor.

I have attempted many times to make myself known to Mrs. Brandon. As the widow of the late Reverend Percy Roberts of Delaford, I believe it would be of immeasurable benefit to our parish should Mrs. Brandon take in hand the necessary formalities attendant on the introduction of a new Rector to Delaford.

I was at first quite certain my letters to dear Mrs. Brandon must have gone astray; but Mrs. Jenkins assured me they had not and that Mrs. Brandon was instead indisposed: I regret to hear of the indisposition of the new lady of the Manor and ask you in her place to accept my sincere good wishes for her speedy recovery.

I shall take it on myself to inform you, Mrs. Ferrars – as I am assured you shall shortly be taking up residence in the Parsonage – of the simple but perennially effective mode of entertainment devised at Delaford for the congregation of our parish.

There will be tea at the Old Rectory on the day of the arrival of the Reverend Ferrars and his wife.

This ceremony, at which the ladies of the parish will present dried nosegays, carved wooden boxes and other crafts over which they have laboured during the long winter months – months, I may add, without the benefit of a Minister to attend the ill or those in danger of losing their faith (when old Ben Frampton departed this world three weeks past, the priest from Honiton was brought in to officiate, the church was quite musty from disuse, and the visiting prebendary most put out that no refreshment was offered after the service).

After tea the brass band from Bridport will play a selection of hymns.

The expected procedure after this would be that I, as widow of the late incumbent, and Mr. and Mrs. Ford of Mapperton Court (who reside without the boundaries of the parish, but have contributed much to the repair of the roof of St. Mary's Church, Delaford) shall dine with yourself and the Reverend Ferrars at the Parsonage.

The fare need not cause much outlay to the Rector's wife: a cold ham and veal pie and some hot soup are all that is anticipated by such as myself – and Mr. and Mrs. Ford will very likely dine in the manner to which they are accustomed, on returning to Mapperton Court.

You will understand, dear Mrs. Ferrars, that it is not my

custom to invite myself to enjoy the hospitality of another.—
It is for this reason that I have tried for so long and in vain
to reach Mrs. Brandon – as, of course, our dearest wish
on coming to the Parsonage for dinner, would be to find
Colonel Brandon and his new young wife included in the
select company.

Domestic arrangements at the Parsonage, which is draughty
and cold at this time of year – and which has, alas! been so
long unoccupied – will be supplied by Meg Cox. If you wish
to inform her in advance of your arrival, she resides at The
Dwellings, Delaford.

Some inhabitants of our little community have found Mrs.
Cox a trifle difficult to handle. But she is, we all believe, a
possible convert to Christianity, should we persevere; and it
is to be hoped the Reverend Ferrars will count amongst his
successes the baptism and receiving into the Church of your
future housekeeper.

Evidence of Mrs. Cox's good heart may be produced in
the form of this fine pair of socks, knit by Meg on hearing
the Reverend's mother was poorly; I enclose them and hope,
dear Mrs. Ferrars, that you do not take umbrage at my
forward behaviour and incorrect invitation to myself and
others to your home.

Yours faithfully,

M. Roberts

Barton Cottage
Devonshire

From Elinor Ferrars to Marianne Brandon

The fourteenth of March 1812

My dear Sister,

I am most alarmed by your last communication to me. I come now, on receipt of it. Do not take any precipitate step, I beg of you, Marianne. You will live to regret it. I shall tell Mama nothing. She remains here with Edward, to keep Mrs. Ferrars from straying up to Barton Park.—

Elinor

Barton Cottage
Devonshire

From Elinor Ferrars to Meg Cox

The fourteenth of March

Dear Mrs. Cox,

I leave Devonshire today to come to Delaford. I should be most obliged if you would air the Parsonage and place blankets on the bed in the room that will be occupied by the Reverend Ferrars and myself.—For the moment, I come alone.

Mrs. Edward Ferrars

From Colonel Brandon to Marianne Brandon

The thirteenth of March 1812

My dearest Marianne,

I write to assure you that my thoughts are never far from you, and from the happy future which lies in store for us.

It is dreary here in the extreme – you would not have found pleasure in accompanying me to the Welsh Borders, where winter has set in with a force barely imaginable in Dorsetshire; and the people, as uncouth as the clime, would not have known how to make you comfortable or to provide you with the little attentions to which your dear mother – and I hope, myself – have made sure you are accustomed.

My news is good, and I will keep this letter brief.

Old Dai Llewellyn, who had long managed the hill farms here, passed away just before Christmas (I did not wish to introduce a subject necessarily gloomy at a time of festive rejoicing round the family hearth) and his son, of whom I had candidly not heard good reports, has turned out a capital fellow: a born estate manager and excellent with the men.

On account of this reassuring result of my visit (and another matter, too delicate to discuss at present, did claim my attention briefly in London before coming down here), I hope and heartily expect to be back with you within the week.

My anticipation, dearest Marianne, sharpens with each hour that passes.—Dear Wife, however aged you may one day become, you will always be the most beautiful woman of that age in the country. Remember this, and take care of yourself – and of our son, whom I know you love already as I do with an ardour and loyalty that will never fade or die.

For yourself, please keep on your flannel petticoats as long as March roars at your windows; do not be deceived by gentle sunshine when a bitter wind comes in from the East as it is wont to do at Delaford at this time of year; and do not on any account undertake any trip to Lyme or elsewhere along the coast. The gales are ferocious, the shingle of Chesil Beach treacherous, and the cliffs, soft and permeable as they are, liable to fall in on any hapless pedestrian who may choose to walk below.

Cherish yourself, my treasured Wife – as I shall cherish you within a few short days, the weather and mire on the roads permitting.

Your loving husband,

Christopher Brandon

From Sir John Thwaite, explorer, to Mrs. Robert Ferrars

The thirteenth of March 1812

Dear Mrs. Ferrars,

We have not met socially, and I can pray solely that you will allow for a communication from a stranger, albeit a stranger returned but a day or so ago from a strange land – a land to which your husband, Robert Ferrars, voyaged in the hope of gaining fame and fortune but met instead the sad fate which I am duty-bound now to recount to you.

I had an expedition set up to journey to the Mountains of the Moon, in Africa, and to travel up the Nile in order to essay to discover the source of that great river along the way.

The King of that remote area, whose friendship I had long cultivated in the hope of gaining information about the diamonds and gold buried deep within his high fiefdom, was introduced to your husband by a missionary just then departing from a thankless seven years' attempt to inculcate the subjects of King Bagra with the life and teachings of our Lord Jesus Christ; and I do believe, on looking back, as I

105

do each day since my long journey home began, that the misfortune which befell Mr. Ferrars stemmed from that introduction. For, by the time I had invited your husband to join our speculative mining venture (Mr. Ferrars pledged a sizeable capital investment, to be sent from England to our camp), the King and his poor, Godless people had imagined themselves now visited by a missionary come to replace Mr. Fletcher, recently left and not lamented, I fear, by any of the Moon tribes.

It was pure exasperation on the part of these savages, I am quite sure, Mrs. Ferrars, and no personal resentment against your husband, that caused the Night of the Long Pig – a festival permitted when tempers run high and drums have beat too long to be ignored by His Majesty.

I cannot describe any further, dear Mrs. Ferrars, the dreadful demise of your husband without causing distress beyond the toleration of an inhabitant of the great country that is England: suffice it to say that, in outrage at the offered banquet and its contents, I departed the Kingdom of Bagra, never to return.

Mr. Ferrars's breeches, tunic and sabre will be sent to you at Ferrars Hall, where I may suppose his dear mother still resides. The short delay will enable you to break the news to Mrs. Ferrars; and, I hope and trust, to come to terms by means of prayer and meditation with the unspeakable manner of death of your late, esteemed husband.

Yours very faithfully,

John Thwaite

The Parsonage
Delaford

From Elinor Ferrars to Mrs. Henry Dashwood

The fifteenth of March 1812

My dear Mama,

I arrived here last night. It is all much worse than we imagined. I attempted to light a fire at the Parsonage, but the old witch who had laid the wood had made a smoky mess of it, so that I was forced to flee out into the muddy lane without so much as lighting a lamp, with dusk falling.

She is not here, Mama! Marianne is gone!

At first I could not believe this to be the case. I walked up the sweep to the Mansion-house; I knocked on the door and was admitted by a housekeeper, very full of suspicion at first. 'Oh, Mrs. Ferrars,' she said. She is new here; Colonel Brandon has hired her especially to guard his precious Marianne; and she had not known me, of course, in the happy days when my dear sister and I were both just wed, and had nought but joy to anticipate, at Delaford. 'Oh Madam,' said poor Mrs. Jenkins, 'I cannot bring myself to inform you of this. I am guilty that I did not follow Mrs. Brandon more closely . . . ' and so on and so forth, but without once vouchsafing any fact, such as poor Marianne's destination. Oh Mama, if my poor sister had been low in spirits and gone to the pond to drown herself, and I too occupied with Edward's mother to stop my own flesh and blood from ending her life—

Mrs. Jenkins did not know any better than I whither her mistress had fled.

Two gowns only were missing, and a light cashmere shawl – and now the treacherous March winds have brought sleet and snow, all the spring flowers which brought solace to my poor sister in her solitude are covered over now and frozen back to death.

We are all distraught. That is, Mrs. Jenkins and the groom here (who has a shifty look about him: I may be able to prise the information from him eventually) and myself.

To make matters worse, an unopened letter, freshly arrived, lies on the hall table. It is from Colonel Brandon: I would know the small neat handwriting anywhere. Do I open the letter, Mama? What shall I do? Do we raise the alarm about Marianne, which will have the whole county gloating and smacking their lips . . . ?

I have seen the postman who promises to entrust this to the Express and we can hear it afar off, on the turnpike road.

Mama, I cannot bear to think we are in part responsible for allowing this cruel blow to descend upon our family.

I shall write tomorrow, as soon as there is news.
Yours affectionately,

Elinor

BARTON PARK
DEVONSHIRE

From Mrs. Jennings to Elinor Ferrars

The sixteenth of March

My dear Elinor,

Your dear Mama has been up to Barton Park in a state of great despair and I have attempted with lime tea and a plate of my best olives to calm her and give her expectations of a better outcome than she can at present imagine.

I fear I have kept from you all what might better have been imparted at the beginning of the year – namely, that John Willoughby of Combe Magna in Somersetshire has been much in the vicinity lately.

I grieve to inform you that poor Margaret has been the subject of his attentions.—I cannot yet determine if he has seduced her, for she cries so long it seems she will drown the whole house with her lachrymosity; but I do know also that the scoundrel has paid court – and in a manner more liable to cause lasting damage than in the case of poor Margaret – to Mrs. Brandon at Delaford, that he has sent her a horse and that she has ridden over to Somersetshire on several occasions to keep a tryst with him.

A marriage broken, a line discontinued in the most appalling way conceivable: for is Mrs. Brandon not with child?—Your poor mother informed me of these expectations not a week ago.

My groom knows of Mrs. Brandon's movements, for his friend in the Delaford stables is well aware of the comings and goings of Mrs. Brandon and her nefarious wooer.

My advice is that you send for Mrs. Brandon at Combe Magna, Elinor. And forgive an old woman for her tact and discretion and simple adherence to those principles of silence and decorum which have for so long dictated the conduct of your friend.

How I wish now I had made public my suspicions. Young women are more of a trial to their elders these days than ever before.

Yours in deepest sympathy,

L. Jennings

May I ask if Mrs. Ferrars is free to come up to Barton Park for a game of Casino tomorrow? She entertains Sir John greatly; and the brood of children here are quite subdued by her presence and general appearance when she comes.

The Parsonage
Delaford

From Elinor Ferrars to Marianne Brandon

The seventeenth of March 1812

My dear, my beloved Sister,

I have learnt from Mrs. Jennings that you are very likely at Combe Magna in Somersetshire, and so I address this to you there – while praying, and hoping against hope you are indeed safe and well, even if living in sin and in urgent need of rescue and return to your home and your wedded spouse.

The pond has been dragged, and also the river at Delaford. The hedges and fields are searched by estate workers here, all under a pledge that they do not bruit this around, for fear of scandal.

Marianne, you have made a grave mistake. Willoughby

cannot give his heart to one woman alone; I hold a secret of his loathsome infidelity – both to his wife, as I must declare and also to you, who were always the standard of perfection to him – but this secret I cannot divulge. You must believe your sister Elinor that this is so; and that, if you were to hear of it the scales would fall from your eyes.—Indeed they would. Your prince would be shown in his true colours. Pray, Marianne, reconsider your over-hasty decision and return to Delaford.

I am here, I, who should months ago have brought company and solicitude to my dear sister; I am here at last in the Parsonage, but a stone's throw from the window-seat where you so long dreamt of perceiving smoke as it arose from my chimney, Marianne . . .

I send on to you also a letter that came when you were already gone. I think it is from Colonel Brandon. Read it with the care and affection a missive from such a man deserves.

Before writing this to you I spoke to the groom here, who I believe has aided you in your flight to Somersetshire.

I pressed him as to Colonel Brandon's visit to Wales, and it all tumbled out: that Miss Eliza Williams, the Colonel's natural daughter, had been housed here on the estate with her bastard child; that the Colonel had taken his daughter to London before placing her in a remote corner of his estates in Wales; and that he, the groom, had been instructed to tell nobody of all of this.

I am certain, my very dear Marianne, that Christopher Brandon, from kindness and delicacy, made a decision to remove his unlawful family on hearing the joyous news that you were to bear a child and heir to Delaford. He did not wish you embarrassed; and all the more so since the father, as you well know, of Colonel Brandon's unlawful granddaughter is none other than the man who brought you almost to death's door last year.—I will not and cannot write his name.

Please, my beloved Sister, return to us here at Delaford. The village needs your laughter, and your aureole of fair hair around your face – like an angel who enchants wherever she goes.

I await your reply at the very soonest, Sister.

Elinor

**The Old Rectory
Delaford**

From Mrs. Percy Roberts to Elinor Ferrars

The eighteenth of March 1812

Dear Mrs. Ferrars,

Please forgive a further intrusion on my part. I understand, however, from signs of habitation evident at the Parsonage that you are at last arrived in our village. May I extend the welcome to yourself and to the Rector which the parishioners have for long reserved for their incoming Minister and his spouse?

May I also be bold enough to enquire as to whether the letter I sent regarding the dinner traditionally given at the Parsonage was received by your good self?

I enquire for the following reason: Framptons the Butchers in Beaminster do an excellent veal and ham pie, and would be able to supply one for Monday, the twenty-first of March, should you place the order with them now.

Please do not think me interfering in your domestic business, dear Mrs. Ferrars. I know it will take you some time to habituate yourself to the ways of our Mrs. Cox; and a ready-made pie would also be extremely acceptable to Mr. and Mrs. Ford of Mapperton Court.

Yours very faithfully,

M. Roberts

We assume the first service at St. Mary's will be conducted by the Reverend Edward Ferrars on Sunday, at St. Mary's?

From Mrs. Henry Dashwood to Elinor Ferrars

The eighteenth of March

My dear Daughter,

I thought of you and pitied you and felt for you at the time of the Ferrars family misfortune, when I should instead have given my attention and affection to poor Marianne. I shall never forgive myself for this neglect.

I come to Delaford at once. We shall endeavour to regain the trust of your poor sister – and rid the country of the scoundrel who has broken hearts and homes wherever he chooses to let his fancy rest.

Edward shall stay here, to care for Mrs. Ferrars. She is distraught – for there is worse tragedy befallen that family, once so high and proud: Robert is eaten by savages, Elinor

– and the news is just come from poor Fanny, who is beside herself, as you may well imagine.

I cannot give time to consider this dreadful event, dear Daughter. It is not made better by the fact that news of Marianne's elopement is out somehow, as well; and Fanny has expressed her determination to visit Mr. Willoughby herself and have the matter out with him. She speaks of him in the same breath as those primitive peoples who boiled her brother: she threatens to take revenge by plunging Mr. Willoughby in a cauldron – and yet again demands the silver and plate which she insists I removed wrongfully from Norland Park, for slicing up the evil-doer and serving him to the inhabitants of Somersetshire.

Between mother and daughter I am at my wits' end, my child. Only Edward shows the deep sorrow fitting to a family bereavement. I leave him here with a heavy heart. I arrive tomorrow at three o'clock.

Your affectionate

Mother

From Marianne Brandon to Elinor Ferrars

The nineteenth of March

My dear Sister,

So you are come at last to Delaford!

I shall miss you there – but you must rest assured of my happiness and contentment at Combe Magna, for we are all in the throes of busy preparation for our life in the New World, and will say farewell to these ancient walls with as much a sense of sadness at parting with the familiar, the dear and the old, as we shall set out with eager anticipation for an existence where equality, love and selflessness will rule the lives of our little community.

We have with us here a red-haired man who plays the guitar very reasonably; his sister in life (for this is how we comrades do term one another, that we may not be possessive of the heart and soul of another being), who is named Adela; two young poets who had tried before to go with S. T. Coleridge to his colony but were thwarted when the Utopia of which the master dreamt did not substantify;

and a half-dozen or so kindred spirits, each one of whom has an agricultural or master-builder's knowledge to his credit, and a vision of a world without greed or patriarchal tyranny that has long burnt in their breasts.

I have understood the meaning of tender love, Elinor. You cannot know it with Edward (though I fear to say this) if you castigate me for my actions.

We are in love night and morn. We eat no meat, and gather spinach and roots from the old kitchen garden – my one fear is we gobble as fast as rabbits, the twelve of us Apostles of the New Purity, and there will be no carrots or radishes left! But the spirits that guide us will provide, just as the fair winds of Spring will carry us safely across the ocean to the wide-flowing Susquehannah, where we shall pitch our tents.

Dear Sister, I fret only for Mama. I leave it to you, and to your sense of what is right for the human heart, to inform her of our sailing. *The Faerie Queen* is near fitted out and our spirits high; once I am gone, Mama must live at Delaford with you, Elinor, for she will be lonesome otherwise . . . but in what way she will understand her new solitary state I am sworn to Willougby to give no indication until such time as we board ship and weigh anchor – Oh happy day!

Write to me of the home I shall never return to: tell me of the old mulberry tree, and the quiet summer evenings in the yew arbour – all when I forward you an address from our commune, Elinor dear.

You are all I shall truly miss. You know it and I weep that I shall see you no more.

Your sister affectionate in life here and for ever,

Marianne

The Parsonage
Delaford

*From Mrs. Henry Dashwood to Marianne
Brandon*

The twenty-first of March

Dearest Daughter,

I am come to be with Elinor, that we may set out together to find you at Combe Magna and return you to Delaford, where you belong.

Your mind is deranged by a pregnancy – with the first time it is not unusual – there are those who eat coal and others who cannot set eyes on their husbands without a desire to vomit. I vow to you, my beloved child, that what you suffer is nothing in comparison with your late grandmother, God rest her soul, who was as much afflicted when the 'French Lady' came as a whole house full of madwomen at Bedlam.—And in pregnancy, indeed in labour.—But I shall not affright you in your delicate condition, my dearest child. Suffice it to say that the joyous moment of giving birth will come; that Colonel Brandon will be at your side; and that together you will regard your infant with all the love of which a contented and happily married couple are capable.

We shall be with you in a few days' time, Marianne. Your loving mother will hold you in her arms again; and you will wonder, as at the time of the fever at Cleveland, what strange dream possessed you.

I bring a cloak, two pairs of thick drawers and all the flannel petticoats so foolishly left behind here – as Mrs. Jenkins has with great sadness informed me.

I cannot be gone from my own home for long. So, dear Marianne, I advise you to accompany me back to Barton Cottage – at the very least until Colonel Brandon is returned from his journey to Wales.

You are in need of a mother's care and attention. Elinor has consented to take in Mrs. Ferrars here at the Parsonage while you stay in your old room, my precious Daughter, surrounded by your own possessions – and indeed some of the books dear Christopher gave to you when you and he first met! You will not feel out of place at Barton Cottage.— And your mother will be happy and reassured by your presence there.

A thousand kisses from your fond

Mama

From Mrs. Robert Ferrars to Edward Ferrars

The twenty-first of March

My dear Edward,

Your mother-in-law is arrived at Delaford, and I have left a card, as I have also done on several occasions to dear Elinor.

No reply comes from either. I cannot bear to think that you grieve alone, or that you have only, as company, the grief of Mrs. Ferrars, who was ever the perfect mother-in-law to me (I fear Elinor and Mrs. Dashwood do not feel for her at all, as I was unable to prevent myself from over-hearing when passing on the other side of the hedge whilst out walking in the muddy lane above the village).

How poor Mrs. Ferrars must suffer – as I do – at the loss of Robert! How you must weep together, without an arm of friendship or condolence about you, without a handkerchief proffered by one who comprehends the magnitude of the disaster which is the un-Christian end of Robert Ferrars.

I come to you tomorrow, Edward. Four long years I held you in my heart; four long years I dreamt each day of our promised nuptials. Who can comfort a bereaved man, who was so long a future spouse, better than his betrothed of yesteryear?

And Mrs. Ferrars, who loves me as her own. I come – by the time you receive this there will be but an hour before my arrival at Barton Cottage.

Your affectionate

Lucy

From Margaret Dashwood to Elinor Ferrars

The twenty-first of March

Dear Sister,

I am laid up so many days at Barton Park I fancy myself to have lost my own family altogether – especially as Mama is now gone to Delaford and I have no close relations in the country.—

Oh, dear Elinor, I need new bonnets and gowns, if only to lift the spirits, even if it is also true my wardrobe is quite threadbare with all the economies you have placed on Barton Cottage, so we cannot eat beef or wear pretty dresses.

But now I *do* need some new hats and gowns – dear Sister, for the sake of your affection for me, can you lend me money to go to Taunton and buy them there? The groom here will convey me, and I shall have time enough for he has some business at the bloodstock market. Please say you will!

I need a different shape for this season: a cap in white sarsenet and lace, fit for carriage wear, for morning; shaped like mine of last year that was satin and lace, shaped round

127

the face with pipes and more fullness and a round crown inserted behind.

Then I shall need large, full bows of very narrow ribbon. And 7 yds rose satin for a fine gown to be made up and measured – but I shall not say where, dear Elinor! That is my secret!

I leave for Taunton next Tuesday in any case. But life would be pleasanter if you would advance me, dearest Elinor, whatever you can spare. The ribbons are two-pence. I do not have any true expectations of the satin for the gown.

Your affectionate sister,

Margaret

Elinor – I cannot be expected to endure life at Barton Cottage with Mama gone and a virago in the form of Mrs. Ferrars running up and down the stairs night and day.

So when you learn I am no longer to be found in Devonshire, do not grieve for me, but celebrate instead my new-found freedom and happiness.

From Marianne Brandon to Elinor Ferrars

The twenty-third of March

My dear Sister,

I have Mama's letter before me. She must not come to Combe. She must not learn of our embarkation for Cythera – that, as you know, dear Elinor, is the island of perfect love to which the ancients sailed.

Neither must you come, dear Sister. I feel ashamed and sad that Mama mourns the loss of me at Delaford; but she must understand that parental rule will be of no significance in our community: the children will care for themselves, and run free, and those who are their elders will in turn feed and clothe the little ones.

For your own peace of mind, dear Sister, and for Mama's, when *The Faerie Queen* has sailed, I advise you not to search high and low for Margaret.—I have asked her to accompany us on this blissful journey. I would not wish to have so pure a heart excluded from our great experiment, and she has accepted – as I knew she would, though she had yearned for

129

her Midsummer Ball and a visit to Mrs. Jennings's house in London, whence she imagined she might go to an opera attended by Lord Byron . . . !

But how could any young person, reared in this land of war-mongering soldiers, carnivores and hypocrites, refuse an invitation to depart for the New World and set up a commune with us? (I have the red-haired guitar player as a possible partner in life for Margaret when she is older: she has a sweet voice and they may lull my dear Willoughby and his Marianne to a sweet sleep in our tent, once our day's work in the fields is done.)

Please inform Mama of this <u>after</u> *The Faerie Queen* has set sail, from Plymouth on the fifteenth of April – Oh fast-approaching, joyous day!

Your affectionate sister,

Marianne

From Mrs. Robert Ferrars to Elinor Ferrars

The twenty-third of March 1812

My dear Elinor,

I know you must wish to be informed of the state of affairs at Barton Cottage. This has been a worrisome time for dear Mrs. Dashwood and for yourself; but the good Lord sends us these trials in order to test the strength of our hearts and minds; and I rejoice to tell you that, through the agency of my comfort and ministrations, both Mrs. Ferrars and Edward can be seen to thrive, and to recover with as much speed as could be hoped for in the circumstances from my husband's sad end.

Elinor, Edward loves you so! Your name is seldom from his lips; and if the presence of a person so familiar to him as myself is more beneficial to him at the present time than that of a virtual stranger (Oh I should not speak in this way of a wife, a soul-mate in the eyes of God), then it is solely because his little ways are as well known to me as my own; I can recall his dislike of rhubarb and so do not attempt to bring it to table; and an hundred other little things, trivial but vital, at a time of bereavement, to the mourner.

Mrs. Ferrars – Bless her heart! – is in fine fettle now the gales and rainy weather of March have passed and she is able to enjoy the garden and orchard as she pleases.

Your Mama's linen is all spread out in the apple trees – it is a harmless conceit, Elinor, and I pray dear Mrs. Dashwood will not object, but Mrs. Ferrars has noted a distinctly musty smell in the linen cupboard and with the aid of Mary we have washed all the sheets and pillow-cases (Jane has left, suddenly, for we know not where).

We have also had the pleasure of entertaining Sir John Middleton to tea.

The charming baronet was most amused to find Mrs. Ferrars in one of your mother's gowns, Elinor! Poor lady, her own wardrobe was savaged by wolves in Norfolk, so she informs me. Right through the meal, for which Mrs. Ferrars produced Mr. Dashwood's best bone china, the pretence was maintained that Mrs. Ferrars was in actuality your mother!—Lord, how we all laughed, and Sir John more than any, at Mrs. Ferrars's excellent rendering of her absent hostess's manner of speech and hand movements &c. 'Anyone would think you had lived years in this cottage, dear Mrs. Ferrars,' said Sir John, as he took his leave. Mrs. Ferrars assures me he has promised to bring the Prince Regent with him next time – but I am not so sure of the veracity of *that*.

Dearest Elinor, we are sisters who grieve the loss of a

brother to your husband and a husband to myself. Forgive us our harmless entertainments.

Yours affectionately,

Lucy Ferrars

Your sister Margaret came to the cottage yesterday. Mrs. Ferrars was packing up the plate in a splendid hamper we found in the attic here – for she tells us it is meant for Fanny at Norland Park and then for her, when her cottage is built at Delaford. But Margaret ran off without so much as giving the time of day.

**The Old Rectory
Delaford**

From Mrs. Percy Roberts to Elinor Ferrars

The twenty-third of March 1812

Dear Mrs. Ferrars,

I was most surprised to hear no bells ring on Sunday from St. Mary's Church.

Are we poor parishioners to suppose the Reverend Ferrars is indisposed and taken to his bed on arrival at the Parsonage?—For I know you are there, dear Mrs. Ferrars: my gardener, who is sent to clip the hedge two days a month, is cursed with a gigantism that makes a ladder unnecessary. I do not encourage him to relate the goings-on in upper windows in our modest and God-fearing village, but he has insisted on relaying to me the fact that he has seen neither hide nor hair of the Rector since you and an elderly lady (your esteemed mother, as we all believe) settled here at the Parsonage.

I trust the Reverend Ferrars has not partaken of Mrs. Cox's pumpkin soup? I reproach myself, if this is the case, with having forgot to warn you. There have been so many small but important matters to attend to, to welcome the new incumbent of the living at Delaford, that this quite escaped my mind.

It is possible that prior social engagements in the county have taken up your and Mr. Ferrars's time, Mrs. Ferrars; and that the Rector, tired from the giddy round, did not find time to prepare a sermon worthy of his first from St. Mary's pulpit. May I remind you, with these lines from Gray's *Elegy Written in a Country Churchyard*:

> Let not Ambition mock their useful toil,
> Their homely joys and destiny obscure;
> Nor Grandeur hear, with a disdainful smile,
> The short and simple annals of the poor.
>
> The boast of heraldry, the pomp of pow'r,
> And all that beauty, all that wealth e'er gave,
> Awaits alike th' inevitable hour:
> The paths of glory lead but to the grave.

We poor parishioners of Delaford would like to be assured of the piety and humility of our new Rector.

I am sure there is a perfect explanation for the echoing sadness of St. Mary's last Sabbath day, Mrs. Ferrars: please do not hesitate to write to me if I can be of any assistance to you at this time.

Yours very faithfully,

M. Roberts

I am obliged to add that I have this very minute received a letter from the town of Beaminster which fills me with shame and self-reproach. I have never been in arrears in paying any bill in my life; and these are family butchers who humbly require payment for their considerable labour and artistry.

In brief, the veal and ham pie was countermanded too late, and is now in my larder. Mr. and Mrs. Ford have departed for their Cumberland estates. I have instructed the butcher to send his note to the Parsonage; and, failing a prompt reply, to the Mansion-house, for the attention of Colonel Brandon himself.

The Parsonage
Delaford

From Elinor Ferrars to Edward Ferrars

The twenty-fourth of March

Dear Edward,

I cannot write to you with affection, though my heart is full.

Come to us here; save poor Mama's things from further despoliation at the hands of Mrs. Ferrars and her acolyte, Lucy. How could you, Edward? How could you?

I begin to think I am wed to a spineless creature, one who cannot make his mark upon the world or follow the precepts of the Church or of his own soul.

If it is necessary, bring your mother here to Delaford. We shall manage somehow. I cannot tell poor Mama

139

of the capers at Barton Cottage – it would break her heart.

Elinor

The Hall
Combe Magna
Somersetshire

From John Dashwood to Mrs. Henry Dashwood

The twenty-fifth of March 1812

Dear Mother,

We are, as you see from the above, at the home of Mr. John Willoughby, Combe Magna (Mr. Willoughby has also lately inherited Allenham Court, the property of Mrs. Smith, who left it – very unwisely we believe – to her relation). He is in temporary residence here before his departure to the New World.

We thank the good Lord that my respected father and your late husband did not live to see his daughter in the menagerie – for there is no other word for it – that is set up at Combe Magna.

Apart from an unsavoury collection of people, some plain ruffians and others so emaciated by their belief in eating nothing but a vegetable regimen that they do not appear to have the strength to cross to Calais, let alone the Americas – there are peacocks that live indoors and strut from room to room, two monkeys from Indo-China or somewhere of

141

the sort; and a donkey that is made as much fuss of as a child would be. It goes about braying stupidly; Fanny's nerves are quite affected by it.

I am come here as head of the Dashwood family and as saviour of my poor half-sister Marianne from this motley band of anti-Christ's disciples. Neither I nor Fanny have had the courtesy of a greeting since we appeared at the house; nor have we been offered refreshment of any kind. Why we are still here will become evident to you as you read on.

At first, when we approached this fine old house, we saw little amiss apart from goats that had strayed on the drive and the sight of a man with an abundance of red hair who sat beneath an oak tree, appearing to serenade thin air, for he played the guitar and sang, but no-one was in sight.

Then our dear sister Marianne ran out of the house. She had espied our chaise and stopped short when she saw us in it: she was overcome with that joy, as Fanny and I both supposed, which visits kinsfolk when once they are reunited after a long and sorely trying absence.

This, alas, proved not to be so. 'What in heaven's name are you doing here?' cried the poor dissolute maiden as we disembarked; and she was joined straightway by the red-haired minstrel, who attempted with all his considerable might to manhandle us away from the porch, despite the fact a light rain fell, and threatened each minute to increase in density.

I did not deign to answer the deranged young woman, but strode into a house still well-appointed (though not as elegantly furnished as Norland Park, naturally).

As I went, a figure dashed past me and made for a room at the top of the stair. 'No, do not go there,' screamed your ill-mannered daughter, dear Madam, as I went steadily on up; and, as if some trick was played on me, found myself in a schoolroom or study quite alone, while the man who had darted past me on the stair had clearly hid himself in an alcove, to make a fool of me.

The young man (and I could see now this was Mr. Willoughby, the husband of the rich Miss Grey, a scoundrel who deserves a thousand floggings for taking her money and stables, as I have heard, and investing all in a crazed community overseas) – this same young man now made to rush into the study after me.

Fanny, from the foot of the stairs, entreated him not to enter. He looked extremely wild. He pushed me aside with extreme violence, and brought Marianne in behind him. 'They wish to separate us, my beloved; but Death shall unite us' – and, before my very own eyes he offered my poor sister a bottle of laudanum. 'By this you can escape from tyranny,' the rogue went on; 'and this (taking a small pistol from his pocket) shall reunite me to you.' Poor Marianne turned as pale as a ghost, and my poor silly Fanny, who is in reality timid at trifles, at the sight of the pistol filled the house with her shrieks. With tears streaming down her face, Marianne entreated him to calm himself and go to another room. 'I won't take this laudanum; but if you will only be reasonable and calm, I will promise to be ever faithful to you.' This seemed to calm him, and he departed from the house, leaving the phial of laudanum on the table.

My dear Madam, I would not bring you to the point of heartbreak with this intelligence if I had not discovered that Mr. Willoughby did indeed leave Combe Magna shortly afterwards. His manservant (if the turbaned creature could be entitled such) informed me his master had gone about Somersetshire to look after some business before departing for the New World; and the redhead, who did at last offer poor Fanny and myself bread and cheese – for the emotions of the past half-hour had left us both speechless

143

and ravenous – contributed the fact that Mr. Willoughby had also various appointments to keep at the White Hart at Taunton, and would be gone several days.

Is this not the time to seize Marianne and return her to her lawfully wedded husband, dear Mother?

Fanny and I have attempted, but to no avail, to persuade my poor sister to leave the attic room where she has locked herself in, at Combe. We shall pass the night here – we have dined on raw spinach from the garden and Fanny will be in need of a visit from our physician when we return to Norland Park.

Where is Colonel Brandon? We are most surprised to find he has not come here with the intention of horse-whipping Mr. Willoughby. I have discovered on the floor of the (unswept) dining-room some lines of verse which I believe must emanate from the pen of Mr. Willoughby. I send them to you, dear Mother: I am distressed to see they are addressed 'To Margaret' and can only pray that I have not two sisters gone crazed for a notorious rake and jilt.

I send on the lines to you, at the Parsonage, where, it is to be earnestly hoped, dear Elinor and Edward lead a life of exemplary virtue and marital fidelity.

> *To Margaret*
> Thy dewy looks sink in my breast;
> Thy gentle words stir poison there;
> Thou hast disturbed the only rest
> That was the portion of despair!

I cannot make out the meaning, though the sentiment is clear enough: the rogue means to wreck the Dashwood family – if these lines are indeed addressed to poor Margaret.

We shall return directly to Norland Park and hope very ardently to hear that Colonel Brandon has taught a lesson to Mr. Willoughby that the young dog will not in a life-time forget . . .

Your affectionate stepson,

John Dashwood

Mrs. Ferrars
requests the company of
Mrs. Henry Dashwood and Mrs. Edward Ferrars
at a Reception
to be held on the seventh of April
at Barton Cottage, Barton Park, near Honiton
at midday

Guests should arrive at half-past eleven in order to form a
line to greet the

PRINCE REGENT

Latecomers will not be admitted.

Carriages six o'clock

Barton Cottage
Devonshire

From Edward Ferrars to Elinor Ferrars

The twenty-sixth of March

My dear – my very dearest Elinor,

I enclose this brief note to you with my mother's card. Oh my Beloved, if you could only know how much I dream of returning to your side. I comprehend so well your feelings and disappointments at the turn things have taken; and I wish sincerely, as you are aware, to take up the living so generously offered me by Colonel Brandon.

But what can I do? My poor mother has lost both her houses, her entire fortune and her favourite son, all within the space of forty days: were I not a firm Christian I would believe a spell had been placed on the family. I cannot leave her side; for each time I talk of leaving for Dorsetshire she throws a fit, and poor Lucy cannot single-handed take charge of her. Lucy is a great comfort to us both here, my love, and I know you will share my gratitude at her self-sacrifice and kindness in bringing us meals and green tea (which, as you know, I cannot stomach, but politeness keeps me from confessing it!) at all hours of the day.—For Jane has left without so much as a word and Mary cannot cook at all.

Elinor, I feel your mother may be distressed to receive this invitation to a party at her own home. But I do recall so well, when first we were wed, that you remarked to Marianne and myself that Mrs. Dashwood, though she kept at a sensible distance from her daughters, was none the less welcome at the Parsonage whenever she might wish to settle there.

Would this not be the best solution, dear Wife? But it must wait until we can talk things over in a civilised manner.

Your affectionate husband,

Edward

What news of your misguided sister?

The Parsonage
Delaford

From Elinor Ferrars to Colonel Brandon

The twenty-seventh of March 1812

Dear Colonel Brandon,

This letter is a very difficult one to write.

I have heard from your housekeeper, Mrs. Jenkins, that you return today to Delaford. By now you will have discovered that Marianne is no longer occupying the Mansion-house; and before the wild talk of the servants adds further to your distress I must tell you, as far as I am aware of them, of the sad details of this affair.

Marianne, I am deeply grieved to inform you, Christopher, has succumbed once more to the blandishments of John Willoughby.

He sent over a horse for her to ride – and despite pleas

151

from Dr. Davis not to mount the animal at this stage in her pregnancy, she was determined on riding over to Somersetshire. And so it all went on.

I take a great deal of the blame, dear Colonel, on my own shoulders, for this sad and scandalous situation.—Had I not kept my own pregnancy a secret as I did, and had I insisted on coming to Delaford to take up residence at the Parsonage, as both duty and desire dictated, I feel certain none of this would have taken place. Marianne would have had a friend – her own loving sister! – to share the pains of her solitude, her apprehension at the coming childbirth, and the hopes for maternal joy that lay ahead of her. But events in the Ferrars family quite overtook us all; and we were stranded at Barton Cottage, aiding and assisting my mother with the unexpected visit of Edward's mother.—I am sure this sounds frivolous indeed, in comparison with the very real tragedy that has descended on you at Delaford . . .

Please do not hesitate to knock at the door of the Parsonage if you would like to discuss this matter. Please, Christopher, let us meet!

With deepest apologies,
Yours affectionately,

Elinor Ferrars

Mrs. Ferrars
requests the company of
Colonel and Mrs. Christopher Brandon
at a Reception
to be held on the seventh of April
at Barton Cottage, Barton Park, near Honiton
at midday

Guests should arrive at half-past eleven in order to form a
line to greet the

PRINCE REGENT

Latecomers will not be admitted.

Carriages six o'clock

Note from Mrs. Ferrars appended:

I am right, am I not, dear Colonel Brandon, to invite your
dear wife to Barton Cottage? Someone somewhere told me
she had run off with somebody.

119 Sloane-street
London

From Mrs. Thomas Palmer to Mrs. Jennings

The thirtieth of March

Dear Mother,

It is still dull as ditchwater here and I daresay little better in the countryside. For all that, I have decided to take the children to Cleveland, that we may pass the Easter-tide there: I shall hand over the infant to the wet-nurse in the village, for all this talk of suckling and going such an inordinate length of time with one's brood has begun to bore me terribly.

Even Mr. Palmer is out of sorts and says he wishes the sun would shine. He has little drollery left in him – save for stealing a lump of meat from Lady Chester's plate the other night and slipping it in her reticule – then crying out as she rose to leave the musical evening, 'Why, there is a piece of rump to end the concert!' – and emptying the poor woman's bag all over the floor so the meat came spilling out. There was much laughter and consternation.

Why in Heaven's name have I received a card from Mrs. Ferrars? I was informed she had lost her wits and was put away in a safe house somewhere: how does she entertain from poor Mrs. Dashwood's cottage? The Prince Regent I know for a fact is at the Pavilion and remains there all April: who does Mrs. Ferrars believe herself to be?

On which topic, I hear all is not well with the marriage of Colonel and Mrs. Brandon. I say 'tis a shame, as I had a letter ready to go off to Mrs. Brandon, suggesting we all come from Cleveland to Delaford to make a change of scenery, but response came there none. I shall go to Taunton with the little ones instead – they have fine Indian jugglers there in the Easter season; and a menagerie with lions and the like: it will be less dull than Somersetshire, that is for certain.

Dear Mother, I feel you must fret without me at Barton Park, but Sir John gets on my nerves so.—Why do you not join us at Taunton and we shall have a fine time away from all the household chores which are the bane of any married woman's life.

Let me know, Mother, by return.

Your affectionate daughter,

Charlotte

From Colonel Brandon to Elinor Ferrars

The thirty-first of March 1812

My dear Mrs. Ferrars – Elinor,

I cannot thank you enough for your kind letter, inspired as it was by none but the sweetest and most affectionate sentiments towards your beloved sister Marianne, while conveying at the same time a sense of reproach against your good self that is wholly unfounded.

It is I, Elinor, who have betrayed that trust which must obtain – nay, grow and ripen – between man and wife: I who went unthinkingly away from the one whom I love more than any being on this Earth, just when I was most needed by her side; I who, believing that all traces of my past love for my cousin Eliza should be eradicated here, and by removing them, removed all hope of future happiness from my life.

I have thought long since I returned to this empty nest, dear Sister, of the steps which might be taken to bring my wife back into the fold, and to prevent – for I have heard the fearsome plan of a voyage and community in the New World from Mrs. Jenkins here (Heaven knows how servants procure their information, but, alas, they do) – a mistaken and perilous journey to a land unimaginably wild and unmanageable for a young woman with the delicate constitution of my wife.

But I cannot bring myself to use force against the precious and perfect person that is Marianne.

She has chosen, Elinor, the man she has long loved – for I know she could be brought to think seriously of me as a husband only after Mr. Willoughby had married Miss Grey – and now they are together, even if their union is not sanctified in the eyes of the Lord, I cannot be the one to put them asunder, sacrilegious though it may be to speak of their lawless marriage in this way.

I love Marianne too much, quite simply, Elinor, to keep her prisoner at Delaford when her heart yearns to be free.

You have, with your usual delicacy, omitted any mention of the child Marianne bears. It is a subject almost too painful for me to contemplate, at present: but suffice it to say that, wherever the child may be born or reared, he shall always be my son and heir to Delaford. I would not cut off an innocent babe from the legitimate expectations that are his by right.

I am told by Mrs. Jenkins that Mrs. Dashwood is at the Parsonage with you.—I thought I would have seen her, but the weather makes walking out too unpleasant for a person of a certain age – though I must count myself amongst such a generation, I confess; and would have done better, I must ruefully accept, to have recalled my years before proposing marriage to poor Marianne.

We shall meet and speak within a matter of days. I try to compose myself here, and to prepare for the day – I am told in the middle of April – when my beloved takes to the high seas, never to return.

Your affectionate brother-in-law,

Christopher Brandon

**The Old Rectory
Delaford**

From Mrs. Percy Roberts to Elinor Ferrars

The first of April 1812

Dear Mrs. Ferrars,

I write to offer my sincere apologies to you, for believing quite wrongly that our new Rector delays showing himself to his parishioners at St. Mary's Church for any other than a deeply religious reason.

May I say, in strictest confidence, that I also am High Church, though I have never dared breathe a word of this. I have comprehended entirely that the Reverend E. Ferrars waits for Palm Sunday to come amongst us.

I anticipate that *Gloria, Laud et Honor* will accompany our Priest, a hymn written, as I am sure you must be aware, by St. Theodulph to celebrate Christ's entry into

161

Jerusalem on a donkey, as described in St. Matthew 21: 1–17.

Mr. Ferrars and yourself, I now realise, with abject and humble sentiments at having misread your secret, will have assigned the opening verses – there are thirty-nine in all – to seven boys, who will be posted at a high spot on the processional route. (I have thought the Brown brothers, Will and Joe, very unusual in their comportment of late, and guarding some knowledge to themselves. Now I know.)

If Palm Sunday is not the chosen time for the appearance of our new Rector, then may I propose the hymn *Come, Holy Ghost, our souls inspire – Veni, Creator Spiritus –* which, as I am once more positive is well known to your respected spouse and yourself, has been variously attributed to Emperor Charles the Fat, grandson of Charlemagne, and Archbishop Mainz . . .

This is generally accompanied by much solemnity and ceremonial, including the ringing of bells, the lighting of candles and the use of incense. It was, of course, used at ordination services and at the consecration of Bishops. I await with breathless expectancy the final choice of the new Rector of Delaford.

Yours faithfully,

M. Roberts

162

From Mrs. Jennings to Mrs. Henry Dashwood

The second of April

My dear Mrs. Dashwood,

I trust you are well settled at Delaford. Here – but I do not know how it is in Dorsetshire – the frequency of showers of rain and bright sunlight have given Lady Middleton a *migraine* and I am once more in charge of my dear grandchildren, who fret dreadfully for want of amusement after this long, dark winter.

It is in the attempt to amuse – or placate – the little ones that I propose a visit to Taunton at Easter, when by all reports Mr. Zormach's menagerie is camped in a field nearby and there are all manner of acrobats, jugglers and other exotic surprises for the distraction of the young.

Dear Mrs. Dashwood, I ask your permission to take your daughter Margaret with us on this expedition. She has been slow to recover from her sprained ankle and heavy cold, and has in any case been asking me most earnestly if she may go to Taunton – if only to examine the new bonnets in the shop-windows, her purse being, as she ruefully confides to me, unlikely to stretch as far as a Spring outfit.

How sad, indeed, Mrs. Dashwood, that your stepson John and his wife are unable to do anything for his sisters. I can only pray that our Midsummer Ball here will provide Margaret with a good match. Though my instincts tell me this may not turn out to be the case. Let us at least hope for a future as secure for Margaret as that promised to your other daughters, so comfortably settled with the Lord of the Manor and the Parson, in one of the most delightful villages in Dorsetshire.

I shall unfortunately not be able to attend Mrs. Ferrars's picnic in the garden of Barton Cottage (I am told she has the rugs and carpets out already, despite the weather) as I shall be at Taunton. But Sir John says he would not miss the fun for anything.

My daughter Mrs. Palmer, who also had the honour of receiving an invitation to the party at your house, will be at the White Hart Inn at Taunton with me and will also have to forgo the pleasure of meeting the Prince Regent.

Your affectionate friend,

L. Jennings

Barton Cottage
Devonshire

From Mrs. Ferrars to Mrs. Henry Dashwood

The third of April

My dear Mary,

I have invited the Countess of Morley to my ball, to be given at Barton Cottage on the seventh of April, but the card has been returned unopened.—Do you have a new address for her?

Also the young man who has been in these parts wooing Margaret while she rests her foot at Barton Park. Oh he is so handsome and delightful; the party would not be the same without him. Is he a celebrity? I think he must be. I have clean forgot his name. Can you supply it? I *must* have him here – though dear Edward shakes his head gravely.

Yours most expectantly,

The Countess Saltmarsh of Ferrars

I have discovered this ancient Scottish title that is mine by right; it descends in the female line. I have informed the Royal party at the Pavilion of the correct mode of address when arriving at Barton Cottage.

**The Old Rectory
Delaford**

From Mrs. Percy Roberts to Colonel Brandon

The fifth of April 1812

Dear Colonel Brandon,

Please forgive an intrusion on your privacy. I have pondered the past day and night whether it would be possible for one such as myself – that is to say, a member of a small Christian community, considered, I may declare with some confidence, to be upstanding in my dealing with the outside world, and aware of the necessity for charity and leniency in cases that might be deemed by harsher judges to be unforgivable – esteemed so highly in this respect, that I suffered many hours of sleeplessness before taking up a pen and addressing the Squire of this same community . . .

Colonel Brandon, it is not my habit to eavesdrop on the conversations of others. In a place the size of Delaford, gossip is already far too prevalent and I have no desire whatever to spread rumour or start idle talk, which can, like wildfire, consume the whole parish in an unimaginably short time.

However, you mother-in-law, Mrs. Dashwood, being gone to Taunton, as Mrs. Cox informed me, whether I would know it or not, I decided yesterday evening to take a pitcher of milk to the door of the Parsonage – the back door, to be exact, for the kitchen, as you well know, opens out on to the cobbles there.

I was but one step from knocking on the back door, to hand in the pitcher of best creamy milk (from my late brother-in-law's herd, but that is another story) when I heard voices inside the pantry, the lattice window on to the back yard being open and there being no way in which a conversation conducted there could go unheard.

At first, Colonel, I experienced an emotion akin to relief – delight and relief, if you will. For many weeks now I had wondered just where the new Rector of Delaford could be. Did he hide himself discreetly in the Parsonage, preparing to guide his flock? Was he indisposed, &c., &c.? And here were the voices of a man and a woman as plain as could be.—

Now, as I say, I was aware of Mrs. Dashwood's visit to Taunton after the receipt of a letter from Mrs. Jennings (Oh dear, the need on the part of Mrs. Cox to impart the most trivial detail is indeed distressing); and so I surmised (as it turned out, quite rightly) that the lady's voice must be that of Mrs. Edward Ferrars, whom I have frequently written to, but alas never as yet entered into the fullness of a correspondence with. Dear Mrs. Ferrars has better things to do than to reply to such as Mrs. Roberts, widow of the late Rector of Delaford.

The man, however—First I saw a white horse tied up at the gate to the back garden – first, that is, after I had come to understand that Mrs. Ferrars's companion was not the Reverend Ferrars, whose likeness hangs in the hall – a sight that cannot be missed by anyone taking the lane behind the Parsonage garden at this time of year to avoid the mud.

The young man of whom I speak, Colonel, was very well favoured; he had a fine figure for a white horse, if I say so myself – and I am no connoisseur of such things, I must hasten to reassure you.

They spoke in low voices, and it seemed the man was pleading for some kind of exemption or understanding from Mrs. Ferrars.

'Elinor,' said he in a beseeching tone so plangent it set the pitcher of milk quivering in my hand, 'forgive me, do! Try to understand my inability to resist . . . my need to inculcate our principles, so strongly held at Combe Magna, and about to be put in practice on the far side of the world . . .'

Such was the tenor of the young man's speech, Colonel Brandon. I heard Mrs. Ferrars reply in a low voice, but with firmness; and I confess I once again experienced relief – for whatever misdemeanour had been committed by the young man on the white horse, it was clearly of a grave nature indeed.

'No, Willoughby, I can never forgive you.' Those were the words Mrs. Ferrars uttered, I am happy to report to you, Colonel. But woe! As she stepped out from the pantry into the passage, and thence to the back door where I still stood very awkward (one such as Mrs. Roberts was not reared at Norland Park in Sussex, with a mother living high on the land that is a baronet and kinsman's, in Devonshire)—woeful it is to me to inform you, Colonel, as brother-in-law to the new incumbent of this living, that Mrs. Ferrars was very pink in the cheek as she came out, and a tear trembled in her eye.

'It is not that I do not wish . . .' and here her voice broke altogether, Colonel, as if she longed to speak her compassion and dared not.

Then the two parted. As soon as they saw me there on the cobbles, the young man went to mount his horse. Mrs. Ferrars looked at me quite distracted, as if she had no need for my pitcher of milk – when I knew very well from Mrs. Cox there was none left at the Parsonage, for Mrs. Dashwood is the one to walk usually to the farm at Four Ashes to collect the daily pitcher. And if she does not go, Farmer Neddy leaves it on the low table by the tree – it was left standing there today, and it was my decision to bring the superior Jersey milk from my brother-in-law's herd, in order to introduce myself in the pleasantest way possible to a new neighbour, the Rector's wife.

But Mrs. Ferrars looked through me as if I were no more than a ghost. Colonel, I fear for her mind, if she is disrupted so entirely by the visit of a handsome young man.—I can say no more.

It is because I have concluded it to be my solemn duty to inform you of this exchange that I write to you now. I also take the opportunity of enclosing a bill from Framptons the Butchers for a veal and ham pie prepared to mark the happy occasion of the Reverend Ferrars's occupying the Parsonage here in the village, but sadly never consumed.

I hope and pray, dear Colonel Brandon, that we shall not have another long wait for a Rector while a couple more accustomed to the felicities of married life are sought all over the county.

Yours very faithfully,

M. Roberts

From Mrs. Henry Dashwood to Elinor Ferrars

The twelfth of April

My dear Daughter,

Margaret is saved!

All was as we had hoped: Mrs Jennings – who returns to Barton Park today and wishes me to convey to you her very sincere sentiments of good will and affection in these troubled times – took me straight to your youngest sister, who waited by a hat-shop in the High Street; I was concealed in an arcade and could look at her, while she could not see me; and sure enough, as we had suspected, Mr. Willoughby appeared on his white horse, dismounted and took her arm as if to lead her into the inn, a groom following behind to take his mount to the stables.

I felt a great sinking and faintness, Elinor, as you may well believe: I think you are the only one of our family to have a steady nerve, for the imaginings of myself, poor Marianne and Margaret have frequently been our undoing; and if we had kept our heads in the first place, we would none of us have fallen prey to poetry and its seductions. It succours me greatly, Daughter, that you have no urge to follow the beliefs or dwell in the fairy kingdom of such as Mr. Willoughby: without you I do not know what we should all do.

Well, we may never see our beloved Marianne again, but we have Margaret safe and sound, and I return to Barton Cottage with her today. (Yes, Barton Cottage, and I shall explain this to you in one minute – I write as fast as the rough nibs and quills of this inn permit me.)

First, my rescue of my child. 'Margaret!' I cried, stepping from the arcade and almost colliding with Mr. Willoughby, who had chosen just that moment to step down from the kerb, the better to assist his most recent prey to walk clear of the mire. 'My Daughter – Mama is here. Oh forgive me, Margaret,' and I burst into uncontrollable sobs, I regret to say, in full view of the thoroughfare.

But our dear little one responded with all the warmth and affection that might be expected of her. After looking around wildly, and calling on me as she had been wont to do when she was ill abed at seven or eight years old, she ran straight across the road and into my arms. We were both weeping profusely . . . I led her into the arcade, and we were a long time staring at some very dull bonnets before we were composed enough to return to the inn, where we climbed immediately to my room and sat many hours talking and crying . . .

Mr. Willoughby did not appear again, Elinor. He has, it appears, been visiting friends and acquaintances in Somersetshire before departing for the New World. Oh that I could have regained two daughters instead of one, and that Colonel Brandon had not expressly forbade any interference with Marianne at Combe Magna, or this would have been the time to go there and cajole her to return to Delaford.

But I have not lost two daughters on the same day. I must

thank the good Lord for His beneficence – even if I must ask Him sternly in future to allow the wishes of mothers and sisters to count for a little more in the world – for if Colonel Brandon had not decreed that Marianne be left alone, and his word is indeed Law as her wedded husband, I feel sure we would have been able at least to make ourselves heard . . .

I must, I repeat, count my blessings, though the loss of one child can barely be counted as such. I have my home returned to me – I know not why or how – I will discover when I am once more in Devonshire. One other good result, I may say, of all this is that Mr. Willoughby cannot molest poor Margaret in Devonshire any longer, for he will be on the other side of the world.

Alas, a thousand times alas! – so will be my poor Marianne.

Perhaps your Edward will come to Delaford at last? Whatever I learn on my arrival at Barton Cottage I will write to you.

Your affectionate

Mother

The Parsonage
Delaford

From Elinor Ferrars to Colonel Brandon

The fifteenth of April 1812

Dear Colonel Brandon,

I have slipped this letter under your door – for I was sorry
not to hear from you earlier.—I know what you must feel,
on this day, the day, as we are both well aware, of the sailing
of *The Faerie Queen* for America, and thus the beginning of
the long – unimaginably long – absence of my dear sister and
your wife, Marianne.

May I come and sit with you? I could distract you a little
with music or cards? – but to mention these pastimes on the
occasion of so tragic a happening as Marianne's defection
does seem frivolous, as I see when I write the words.

I could sit with you in silence, Christopher. We are both

perhaps better at concealing our thoughts and feelings than expressing them.

Please let me know what you would like and I will immediately comply with your wishes.

Your faithful friend,

E. F.

Mulberry Cottage
Delaford

From Mrs. Robert Ferrars to Colonel Brandon

The sixteenth of April

Dear Colonel Brandon,

We are only slightly acquainted – I am the widow of the late Robert Ferrars, who was recently and tragically eaten in the Bush – and I am at present at my sister's house: she is Mrs. Davis, wife of the physician who, I believe I am right in stating, attended Mrs. Brandon before she departed from Delaford.

I have just returned from a visit to my mother-in-law at Barton Cottage; I would have stayed longer than I did, had it not been for the outcome of the party held by Mrs. Ferrars there last week.

I think dear Edward – to whom, I should confide to you, I was affianced four years at Plymouth before Miss Dashwood appeared on the scene – was as surprised as I by the very great success of our humble picnic at Barton Cottage.

It is true, the sun shone throughout, which gave the rugs and carpets placed days before on the grass by Mrs. Ferrars a chance to lose some of the aroma which had pestered us over the preceding period, and I cannot desist from congratulating myself on the griddle cakes and other delicacies presented on that day.

I could not have anticipated, however, the vast success of Mrs. Ferrars herself with the Prince. I do not think Edward knew where to look.—They were a long while in the shrubbery and then were playing hide-and-seek in the cottage (though there are not many places to hide there!) – and the party went on until well after dusk, when Sir John had us all up to Barton Park; he has the acquaintance of the Prince, who was keen to further the same as a means of spending more time with Mrs. Ferrars.

In short, Colonel, Sir John then and there offered Mrs. Ferrars a cottage on his estate – it is several miles from Mrs. Dashwood's, which I am sure that good lady will much regret, for the fashionable cottage will in future, thanks to the promised visits of the Prince, be Mrs. Ferrars's cottage. I am invited as one of the very first guests.

For the time, however, I find myself at Delaford. I make no direct allusion, naturally, to your recent tragic loss, but I would like you to know that I am ever available for company of an evening; and that I have already baked a batch of griddle cakes, adding on this occasion, as I did at Barton Cottage, an ingredient supplied by Meg Cox of this village, which promises to allay pain and provide happiness on ingestion.

Dear Colonel, I feel we should permit ourselves this opportunity to become better acquainted: as Sir John Middleton remarked, when your abandonment and solitude were spoken of at Barton Park, we are almost related, for my late husband was brother-in-law to your absent wife.

I remain, dear Colonel Brandon,
Your faithful servant,

Lucy Ferrars

Barton Cottage
Devonshire

From Edward Ferrars to Elinor Ferrars

The seventeenth of April

My dear Elinor,

I write to beg your forgiveness, my beloved Wife.

For too many years I have obeyed my mother's instructions and placed her first in my affections, as it seemed right a devoted son should.

When her estates and fortunes were lost, I felt all the more keenly for her; and when it appeared she had lost her wits to boot, my heart was full of sympathy and tender concern for the one who brought me into the world.

Despite the fact that she disinherited me in favour of my younger brother, my loyalty was still above all else to my mother.

Only when Lucy Steele – as I shall ever know her – came to the cottage, and I saw a connivance between the two women, that I should desert my beloved wife, surrender my living at Delaford and deny my vocation as a Minister of the Church, did I understand how far I had strayed from the path of righteousness – and, it goes without saying, the path of my true love.

Can you forgive me, Elinor? I return tomorrow to Delaford, and pray you will at least grant an audience to

Your loving husband,

Edward

I am relieved to inform you that Sir John Middleton has made a gift of an excellent cottage to my mother. She has asked him to construct a pavilion for her in the garden.

Now – just as I was about to seal this to you – news, unimaginable news: a letter to your Mama here – from Marianne!

Yes, from your sister! She also begs forgiveness.—Oh, how she and I have both sinned, in the eyes of the Dashwood family and the world at large! She writes from Delaford.

Marianne is returned to the Mansion-house, Elinor. Does she not come to you? How does the Colonel feel at her return? Your mother is beside herself with joy and astonishment . . .

Edward

Delaford House
Dorsetshire

From Marianne Brandon to Elinor Ferrars

The seventeenth of April

My dear Sister,

I came here yesterday. I could not give you the news immediately for there is some suggestion – quite absurd, I know – that you have entertained none other than John Willoughby at the Parsonage and have therefore shown a preference for his views on life and on morals and general comportment over those of my dear husband.

Naturally, I did not believe any of this.

I wish you simply to know that I am the happiest and most fortunate woman on Earth.

When Mama wrote to me at Combe Magna and told me of poor Margaret and her seduction by the one to whom I

183

had promised eternal faithfulness, I understood at last. (Oh, how patient you have all been with me!) For tyranny is not the portion of my dear husband. Christopher left me to discover my own heart, and the error of my ways. He has had the liberal approach to all I do and I have chosen of my own free will to return to him.

The tyrant is Willoughby, who binds women to him body and soul in the name of ideals and poetry, and then casts the human husks aside when once the flesh is consumed.

We shall all be happy together here, dearest Elinor. Shall Edward come to Delaford soon? I have been too selfish to pay attention to the troubles he has undergone with Mrs. Ferrars . . . I have chased a dream, rather than the reality of love.

This I cannot describe to you, but I know, dearest Sister, that you love also, though your way is very different from mine.

I can only say that, if you had seen Christopher's face when I walked into the long library where he sat by the fire alone; if you could have felt his stillness, his quiet joy, the depth and sincerity of his forgiveness of me – you would have wept, as I did, at the strange beauty and tranquillity of true love.

I shall come to the yew arbour tomorrow, rain or shine. Please, dear Elinor, come and meet me there.

Your affectionate sister,

Marianne